– 1 –

YASEMIN'S DESPERATION

One voice among thousands

Nurgül Sönmez

Bibliografische Information der Deutschen Nationalbibliothek: Die Deutsche
Nationalbibliothek verzeichnet diese Publikation in der Deutschen Nationalbibliografie;
detaillierte bibliografische Daten sind im Internet über http://dnb.dnb.de abrufbar.

Die automatisierte Analyse des Werkes, um daraus Informationen insbesondere
über Muster, Trends und Korrelationen gemäß §44b UrhG (Text und Data Mining")
zu gewinnen, ist untersagt.

© 2021 Nurgül Sönmez

Lektorat: Arzu Kaya
Korrektorat: Meryem Yıldırım
Weitere Mitwirkende: Gamze Taşdemir

Verlag: BoD · Books on Demand GmbH, Überseering 33, 22297 Hamburg,
bod@bod.de
Druck: Libri Plureos GmbH, Friedensallee 273, 22763 Hamburg

ISBN: 978-3-7693-0853-2

Imprint

YASEMIN'S DESPERATION – 1

Originally translated from German, published in 2022 ©

Nurgül Sönmez

Translation: Nurgül Sönmez
Compilation / Editor: Arzu Kaya
Final Check : Meryem Yıldrıım
Book Cover Design: Gamze Taşdemir
Illustration / Index: Gamze Taşdemir

Author Contact Information:

M ns.nurgulsonmez@gmail.com

🅕 nurgulsonmez

🅞 nurgulsonmezofficial

Team:

g.tsdmrr@gmail.com

To all book lovers...

Biography

Nurgül Sönmez

21.08.1979
Germany

In the years between 1995-2020, she often received awards.

She began writing in 1995 and has written countless poems,

song lyrics and novels. Written based on true events.

The rights to over 50 novels and over 2500 song lyrics were taken over

by various publishers and famous composers.

Now she no longer stands behind the scenes,

but with her works in the middle of the stage.

Nurgül Sönmez
– Schriftstellerin –

AUTHOR'S WORKS

- Her first book ANA (Poem - Turkish) was published in **2014**
- **2015** YASEMİN'İN SAVAŞI (Turkish)
- **2017** YASEMİN'İN İNTİKAMI (Turkish)

2021

- Matilda (Turkish, German)
- 1001 GECE YERİNE - BİN BİR GÜN (Turkish)
- STATT 1001 NACHT - TAUSENDUNDEIN TAG (German)
- YASEMİN'İN ÇARESİZLİĞİ 1 (Turkish)
- YASEMİN'İN SAVAŞI 2 (Turkish)
- YASEMİN'İN İNTİKAMI 3 (Turkish)

2022

- Matilda (English)
- YASEMINS VERZWEIFELUNG 1 (German)
- MAAROUF (Turkish, German)
- INSTEAD OF 1001 NIGHT - THOUSAND AND ONE DAY (English)
- YASEMINS KAMPF 2 (German)

2023

- YASEMINS RACHE 3 (German)

2024

- YASEMIN'S DESPERATION 1 (English)
- YASEMIN'S STRUGGLE 2 (English)
- YASEMIN'S REVENGE 3 (English)
- MAAROUF (English)

All books have been translated into French and are planned for future book projects. This will be followed by translations into Arabic and Spanish. If there is interest and demand, there will also be translation in other languages.

Her works © are based on true events and she continue to support social projects with the proceeds of the books.

Soon also available as audiobooks!

Nurgül Sönmez
– Schriftstellerin –

Thousands of voices can be hope for a voice.

Based on a true story!

Desperation!

Yasemin is 21 years young, breathtakingly beautiful and her eyes are like the blue of the sky.

Nevertheless, her eyes are filled with sadness and suffering. A suffering that is hard to endure and hard to imagine for one person alone.

Tyranny, torture and fear of death. Yasemin faces all of this on her way. She encounters unimaginably evil people. The kind-hearted people who are like a light for her give her all the more strength.

Will she win the fight?
Will she manage to free herself from despair?

CHAPTER
1

Yasemin hadn't come to work for a week, although she wasn't ill. I was very worried about that. So I wrote her a message. After a full four and a half hours of waiting, I finally got an answer: "Nurgül, I'll call you at 9:30 p.m., then I'll be alone. Don't call or write. Enough is enough! I did not deserve that. I'm so exhausted I can't take it anymore!"

My co-worker's message startled me and I started thinking about her. I was expecting the time to go faster until 9:30pm, but it just wouldn't get any later. I paced the house like I'd committed a serious crime. I said to myself, "I hope nothing happened to her."

Her message finally came at 9:47 p.m.: He didn't go to work. I'll try to get in touch later. "Yasemin! Tell me what happened right now. If you need help, don't be afraid. Please talk to me" I texted her back. Worried, I didn't fall asleep until morning. I waited all night for an answer. At around six in the morning I finally received a text message from Yasemin: "I'm coming!" I sighed with relief.

When my brother woke up, I prepared breakfast for us. Actually, I need a cup of tea, but I didn't get around to it. Suddenly the door kept ringing. I ran to the front door in fear and panic. It could only be Yasemin, why did she ring the storm?

Yasemin was standing in front of my apartment. Her tearful, blue eyes stared at me, her hug meant something like "Saved at last". I didn't even notice her two siblings because I was so happy to see them and only focused on them.

From a young age, Yasemin took care of her two siblings. Her brother Suat was eleven and her sister Kiraz was seven years old. The responsibility was on Yasemin's tiny shoulders, which grew every day. She was even ready to sacrifice her life to protect her two siblings.

Up to this point we had never shared our private lives. We respected each other's privacy because we were afraid of hurting each other. We agree on not sharing more details.

Yasemin and her siblings didn't even have time to drink tea that day. My beautiful heroine, in a hurry to take her siblings to school, hid tears from them. She stood in front of me, exhausted. It was like seeing a reflection of my own life in front of me. At that moment I thanked my Lord and fled back to HIM.

There was no mother and father, maybe I didn't know, maybe they do, but they weren't there at that moment. She was like both mother and father to her siblings. Yasemin made up for their lack. Even though she didn't say it, that day, that moment, I felt and saw it by living it.

The three looked as if they had escaped from home. I braced myself for anything and was alarmed. But there was no time to talk. So I quickly prepared a lunch box for the kids and gave it to them. »Thank you Nurgül!«, Yasemin said and kissed my cheeks. She was in a hurry to get down the stairs to take the kids to school. Raising her voice, she called up from the bottom step, "I'll call you at lunchtime."

That relaxed me a little. However, I didn't feel good at all. I didn't know what happened to her. The most important thing was that she was responsible for her siblings. No matter what happened, she tried and resisted. I appreciated that she trusted me so much. Yasemin! My strong, determined heroine, who took care of her siblings. I understood that Yasemin had been through a lot, but I didn't exactly know her life story. Despite that, she was still a heroine to me. She was hardworking, compassionate and responsible, loving almost like a "MOTHER". What was normal for her, didn't seem so to others.

I had endless faith in Yasemin because she wasn't acting. She wasn't an actress, not even the leading lady in her own life. She fought a hard struggle with her living conditions. She did all this for her siblings, not for herself.

They are the lines of silent scream,

Jasmine.

Yasemin's Desperation

CHAPTER
2

The promised message from Yasemin that she wanted to send me in the afternoon didn't come. Did she at least call work? Without further ado I wrote to my boss from the hairdressing salon, because this question was always buzzing around in my head and gave me no peace. I was sad because the answer was negative. My eyes rested on the clock, but my thoughts were on Yasemin. I was surprised because I remembered what she wrote yesterday: "Don't write, I'll write to you." Did that mean she was afraid of someone? My shift at the restaurant was over. I couldn't make ends meet with a job. I went home after my daily shopping. Yasemin and her siblings were waiting for me in front of my door. I approached them with quick steps. My only desire was to find out what was going on. She was happy to see me and approached me with a bitter smile. "Hello, I couldn't inform you. He took my phone away" she apologized. It was as I suspected, Yasemin was terribly afraid of someone, even very scared. The situation was self-explanatory. She was already in a difficult situation.

"Come on, let's not talk outside, let's go inside. Then we tell each other what there is to tell. Did you already eat? Are you hungry?" I asked as we climbed the stairs. "I'm not that important, but my siblings couldn't eat after school," Yasemin replied.

As soon as I entered the house, I rushed into the kitchen, put the shopping bags on the table and greeted the three of them with a loving hug. "Welcome, I'm very glad you're here," I confessed.

Then I told them, "Come on kids, wash your hands while I put the groceries in the cupboards." They both listened, so they replied, "Okay." Then they went into the bathroom. "Yasemin, what's the matter? I respect your privacy. Even though I don't know anything about you, I trust you, I believe in you! You are in a difficult situation, you are scared and afraid of someone. Please tell me what's bothering you, but not in front of the children," I challenged her. Her jaw started shaking and her eyes filled with tears. I hugged Yasemin who couldn't contain her emotions. Her tears ran in streams down her cheeks. I rested her head on my shoulder caringly, then stroked her hair. Her crying got louder and she started sobbing.

When I heard the bathroom door and the children approached the kitchen again, I called them to order: "Come on! Now is the time to be strong." I quickly ushered the kids into the living room, leaving Yasemin in the kitchen. I didn't want the boys to worry and see the tears. The siblings conveyed to me that they trusted me, that they were in good hands and that they felt comfortable. Of course I was very happy about that.

After sitting on the couch, I asked, "What did you guys do at school? Do you have homework?" They both talked at the same time: "Yes, we have." "Okay, then you do your homework now. In the meantime, I'll prepare dinner with your sister," I replied with a smile. In the kitchen I stood next to Yasemin. Finally we had the opportunity to speak for the first time. I wanted to listen without breathing so I didn't miss anything. Even if we didn't have much time, we had to take the moment.

Yasemin immediately told about her life. She was born in Türkiye. She lost her mother at a young age. Excitedly, she spoke in short, half-sentences that her life had changed completely after the death of her mother. Even though I didn't know her life story, it was like seeing my face in the mirror. Although we have hardly had an intimate conversation up until now, I had a deep feeling that we would find common aspects and parallels to each other. My suspicion was already confirmed with your first sentence. She had no mother ...

Yasemin used to live in Türkiye, she grew up as an only child. Her parents earned their living by selling everything they harvested from the fields and vineyards and offered at the market. "When I was ten, I started working as a hairdresser's assistant in our community," said Yasemin, who loved reading but left school after fifth grade because she needed to earn money.

The manual skills were her, she was very skilful in this job. After the death of her mother, she struggled with the pain and loss. Nevertheless, the reading lover took care of the obligations of the house. She tended the gardens and fields, in addition she continued to work in the barber shop.

In her childhood she bore the heavy and great burden of responsibility that she actually could not bear. In between I looked after the children. They sat in the living room and did their homework. So Yasemin continued to tell me her life story in short sentences. Catastrophic and terrible changes happened in her life after her father remarried two months after her mother's death. Yasemin's stepmother had a terrible character like the evil stepmothers in movies. With tears, Yasemin showed me her wounds on her body.

They were striped and also circular deep scars. With a trembling voice, she described the cruel violence and the marks that her stepmother had inflicted on her. I didn't want to put her in psychological distress, even for her to tell the details. As a person who is always opposed to violence, I am in favor of spreading tyranny openly. As a child, Yasemin didn't even have a girlfriend. Due to her work and responsible life, she never found time to socialize with other children.

Yasemin, who couldn't even make friends with herself, suddenly said: "I wanted to be a prosecutor. I wanted to protect the victims from injustice, and also establish legal sanctions for those who committed crimes." The bright light in her eyes still floated in my mind. It was indeed an expression of how much injustice had been done to her. The Yasemin sitting in front of me had both feet on the ground, reaching for life with her hands in order to partake of it. The woman I saw was not a weak person. The pain and injustices she experienced made her a strong character and this is Yasemin. "I've been a mother to my half-siblings since they were born. They grew up in my hands. I cared for them and raised ," she said, making my heart ache at that moment. Little Yasemin, it was a very mature life that she had to live in her childhood. It was inhuman, but part of the reality of life, of thousands of similar cases.

The warm meal was eaten and the children's hunger was satisfied. We had ended the intensive conversation and didn't want to continue it in front of Yasemin's siblings. She kept glancing hastily at the clock, and when she looked out the window, she slowly became restless. It seemed like she was only allowed to be away from home for a certain amount of time. She acted like she had to go home before the person who was scaring her came to get her. I asked her in a worried but calm tone that gave her confidence, "Yasemin, with whom do you live under the same roof? Who took your phone and why? Why are you so hectic?" The young woman replied, "We live with my aunt. When my father died, my stepmother left my siblings to me. We actually live with my paternal aunt, but it's a long story. I'll tell you about it another time." She quickly hurried to help her siblings into their shoes and jacket.

Talking had relieved me, but it had also been draining as I felt like I was carrying a very heavy load on my shoulders. We hugged as she said, "My sick leave is through the end of this week. In the meantime, I have many things to do, my siblings and I should live in peace. I'll be back at work next week and try to get my phone back.If it doesn't exist, I'll secretly buy a new one."She explained that there was a fight in the house, perhaps she was still at the mercy of the violence. Yasemin's painful days were not over. She still carried the same pain with her. Yasemin was at war and struggling. Even though she was tired and exhausted, before she left the house she was a completely different person, a completely different personality. With her appearance, she had a strong and hard structure, as if no one was allowed to approach her. Her body language signalled that she wanted to protect herself from society.

I watched the three of them until they disappeared from view. Her life story was somewhat similar to mine in some respects. So I could empathise with her. I understood, even if she didn't say it, and everything I suspected was confirmed.

"Words" became the sound of silent screams.

Yasemin's Desperation

CHAPTER
3

"Yasemin was an orphan."

After the death of her father, her stepmother ran away from home. She left the children to Yasemin. But Yasemin was still a child himself and was left alone with the little ones in the village house made of clay, which had only two rooms. Despite suffering tremendous shock, resilience and fighting spirit helped her stay alive.

What had she experienced and seen in her teens? I thought about it and sighed deeply. Her short story, which she told me through tears and horror, had hit my heart hard. Injured Yasemin!

While Yasemin was about to blossom like a flower, people around her even tried to turn off the water and tear off the leaves to make them fade. But she fought back, didn't give up, was strong enough to blossom, to open like a flower. She fought despite the injuries she carried.

Although days had passed, I did not receive the slightest message from Yasemin. Her siblings also seemed invisible. I didn't see her go to school. "I hope nothing happened to them," I sighed inwardly, then began to worry. My boss was a nice person. We got along very well with her. In our free time, we often met with her to go out for a meal or something to drink too. Yasemin opened her heart to me, I definitely didn't tell my boss what she said. 'Cause what she told me, was a secret between us and I didn't want to lose her trust. So I had to find another way to reach Yasemin.

Yasemin only did an internship in the hairdressing salon where we worked together. She could do everything this job required. She even did more than she had to. Encouraged by my boss's sincerity, I asked, "You know that Yasemin is hardworking and determined. She hasn't called in for days and I'm worried about her. The address is definitely included in the internship contract. What do you say, boss, let's buy a bouquet of flowers and go to her house?"

"That's a very good idea," she replied, making me very happy. At the end of the working day, the three of us made our way to Yasemin. I was worried, excited and the truth was, even a little scared. Of course, my intention wasn't bad. I didn't want to betray my boss like that. I would never do that, and I didn't think I had. Because she really was an optimistic and compassionate person. But our project excited me and scared me. On the way to Yasemin's we had a nice chat and suddenly we laughed. But suddenly I had doubts.

Oh no! What had I done? What if the people she lived with didn't know she was on sick leave? What if I unintentionally put her in an even more difficult situation than now? Oh my god what had I done? Somehow I had to explain this to my boss and colleagues, but how? While my intention was good, I was afraid to do evil without realizing it.

"What if we harm her with this visit?" I voiced my thoughts simply. My boss said, "We won't say anything, just that we want to surprise her." My boss was an angel. She was very human. Without asking any questions, she acceded to my request to visit Yasemin. Although she knew she was in a difficult situation, she immediately agreed without asking any questions. She insisted on checking on Yasemin: "We're here now, we're not going back." My heart began to beat faster. What image would I come across? I sincerely hoped that our unannounced visit would not harm Yasemin and her siblings!

My boss rang the doorbell and my hands started sweating like I was going to an interview. I rubbed them together as I climbed the stairs. Little Suat shyly opened the door. "Hello, Nurgül!" he greeted me and opened the door a little more. A very hard, loud, and commanding voice yelled from the background, "Who are these people?" When we heard someone's firm footsteps approaching the door, Suat, my boss, my colleague, and I looked at each other in concern. Suddenly the door swung fully open. Our eyes were wide and I started to swallow in fear. Suat disappeared from view as the man viciously pulled him away from the door by his t-shirt. In front of us was a nervous, irritable man with a moustache. At that moment, I frowned curiously and took a step back. "Who are you?" he barked at us. I swallowed again and pointed my hand at us. "Well, we're Yasemin's colleagues, and this is our boss. We're the hairdressing team she's doing an internship with," I explained.

Again my boss stood up for us as the man's testy body language hardened. As a German, she knew a little Turkish and spoke with her broken knowledge of Turkish: "Yasemin is a good employee, she does an excellent job. We're here to congratulate her. Are you the father?" My boss hadn't betrayed Yasemin. In his loud and hard voice he roared, "No, I am your aunt's husband. She has something to do now, she can't come to the door." My boss gave the flowers and the chocolates to the man. He took the gifts gruffly, then slammed the door in our faces. We were shocked! All three of us gasped at the same time and stared at each other for a few seconds, "What was that?" I can't remember coming down the stairs. I was horrified and in shock, as was my boss, who then suggested, "Let's go have a drink. We'll talk after we've calmed down."

Without being picky, we stopped at the nearest cafeteria. All the tables were close together and we sat down. Everyone took a deep breath. "What was that?" we spoke at once and began exchanging our ideas and thoughts. My boss felt responsible for the situation and was upset. Her urge to help grew and she asked, "What should I do? What should we do?" Yasemin and her siblings were in a difficult situation and my boss asked about the little boy. "He was her brother," I replied. I didn't say more because Yasemin had trusted me, so I couldn't reveal what she had told me. Even though I was dying to share her story, I kept quiet because I was afraid I would hurt Yasemin. After all, she hadn't trusted anyone before me and kept her secret to herself. I felt honoured.

The three of us were very confused and desperate. We didn't know what to do in this situation. The way we walked up to her together laughing and how bitter, confused and desperate we came back from her was terrifying. As I sipped my last sip of coffee, I received a message from a number that wasn't on my phone.

"It's Yasemin. I can't thank you enough. Thank you for not betraying me. Otherwise I would be very badly off. I'm trying to get custody of my siblings. That's why I'm on sick leave. I sincerely apologise to my boss. I'll tell her everything when I come to work next week. I'm glad to have met you. I'll turn my phone off again."

The message was translated into German and I read it out. My boss immediately offered: "I've already noticed that something isn't going well. If she texts you again, you can give her my cell phone number. She can call me if she gets into trouble." So we all left the cafeteria, exhausted. There wasn't much time left until Friday evening, and the next week was fast approaching. My brain had stopped working, I was all confused. Yasemin's problems had now become mine.

"Everyone makes the right decision for themselves. No one has the right to dominate another's life or make decisions about it. Nobody has the right to do that! We all have the freedom to make our own choices, to choose our own lives, and to exercise our own free will. Someone else can't have that right, it shouldn't be! "

Nurgül Sönmez

CHAPTER
4

Although I haven't known Yasemin for long, I took her wounds into my heart. Even my boss had no doubts about her words, because Yasemin spoke the truth. She spoke with a sluggish, bitter mood and it was really REAL! She hadn't lied!

It was just after 8:45 a.m. I was late Yasemin had been waiting in front of the hair salon since 8.30 a.m. and got to the entrance before me. That's what I thought, but there just wasn't a Yasemin when I showed up at our meeting point. I watched the path, but there was no sign of her. Our girls rolled in. Although my boss was on leave for the day, she came anyway. It was after nine o'clock, but there wasn't a Yasemin in sight.

We let customers in with or without an appointment. We're all busy with our work, it's been a shambles while we're looking for Yasemin. We looked at each other with hopes of a bright future and couldn't really focus on our customers. I will never forget this day. The time had stood still for me, the conversation with the customers felt like a heavy burden for me. We continued to watch the street, it was already approaching 11:00 a.m. There was still no sign of Yasemin. My boss couldn't take it anymore and blurted out: "That's enough! We'll call the number she used to text you!"

I only knew a fraction of her story but my boss knew nothing about her and yet she was human and compassionate. Yasemin had conquered our hearts! We called them but the phone was off. So we all just kept waiting at the hair salon. It was 3 p.m. There was still no news from Yasemin. At around 3:40 p.m., a police vehicle pulled up in front of the hair salon. We all looked startled. Yasemin got out of the police vehicle, intimidated and scared. She looked tearful, her hair was disheveled and her shirt was torn. She quickly ran into the living room.

Normally there were never any difficulties with Yasemin, she was careful with her customers, but today she just let herself go. Her face was wet with tears and she was in a miserable condition. Our boss ran towards her and shielded her immediately. Although she had only been in Germany for five years, she spoke fluent German. She cried out and cried, both with joy and pain. The hair salon was crowded. We didn't care, each of us left their client and we rushed to Yasemin. She didn't have anyone. There was no knocking door to go to. She was all alone! Carrying the responsibilities of her siblings on her shoulders, she successfully completed whatever task life throws at her. She had conquered my heart. My angel ...

The police officer asked, "Are you Ms. Nurgül Sönmez?" "Yes, I am!" I confirmed. " Please!" Yasemin cannot and does not want to stay in this city anymore because of the terrible events that she and her siblings went through. It's for your own safety. She wants you with her. Would you like to come with us?"

the officer asked. "Of course I won't leave her alone, I'll come with you!" was my answer. My boss angel agreed: "We won't leave Yasemin alone." We immediately got into the police vehicle and drove to the police station. Yasemin, whose head was resting on my shoulder, continued to cry bitterly. I stroked her hair to comfort her and promised that I would stay with her so that she no longer had to be afraid.

Yasemin sobbed: "I finally made it! We survive!" What did she mean? She didn't tell even a quarter of what had happened to her. What I knew was nothing.

The true story begins from now on....

Silence;

Speak so that mankind will not die!

Yasemin's Desperation

CHAPTER
5

After a short while we arrived at the station. Suat and Kiraz ate sandwiches given to them by the police. A growl of hunger came from Yasemin's stomach as well. "Yasemin," I admonished her. But she replied: "Let them eat, when they have satisfied their hunger, I will be full too." She always put the well-being of her siblings before her own.

It wasn't clear where we were going. We didn't get a chance to talk because her siblings were with us. I pulled her aside. 'Just give me a little bit of what's going on. Did you receive a criminal complaint? What happened? Tell me! Don't be silent!' I begged her. I showed her in words that I meant it. She couldn't even look me in the eye. She hugged me crying and sobbing again: "What hasn't happened over the years? how can i explain it to you I can not say it! I am ashamed! How can I tell you?" She slipped out of my arms, clutching weakly around my neck, she repeated over and over, then passed out!

The officials rushed over immediately after my call for help. To my horror, Yasemin hadn't passed out, she was having a fit. White foam spurted out of her mouth, her eyes fluttered. Her pupils were twisted. I ran to her siblings and hugged them both. I quickly turned my back on the terrible situation to distance her siblings from this painful scene. At the same time I tried to calm her down.

The two younger siblings, not knowing what was happening to their sister, went mad with fear and started crying. Only 21 years old, Yasemin had a seizure after accumulating pain and torture over the years.

The ambulance came very quickly, they immediately provided first aid on the spot. They then took her to a hospital in an ambulance. I didn't go because I didn't want to leave the children. The police escorted her and I didn't have to worry anymore, she was in good hands. I followed the ambulance with my siblings in a police car.

It was getting pretty late and darkness was falling. We sat in the hallway across from Yasemin's room. She was on an IV and asleep. Due to the medication she was given, she kept dozing off. Since there was nothing more I could do, I gave my number to the hospital and the police. I took the two children with me that evening and took responsibility for them. The police officers who took us to the train station had it confirmed in writing. "If anything happens, call 110 immediately!" they told me and then drove away. When they got home, the children took a shower one by one, they were exhausted and tired from the hard day. They weren't hungry, so I prepared their sleeping places for them, and they fell asleep immediately.

After calm had returned, I called my boss, who had already tried to reach me several times. I told her everything from start to finish. "You did well by taking the children with you. I'll pick you up tomorrow morning around 7 a.m., then we'll drive to Yasemin's. You don't have to work tomorrow, don't leave the siblings alone!" she offered me. I was very grateful to her because I was battered by the intensity of the day and tired from what had happened. So I prepared a bed in the same room where the children were lying and fell asleep immediately.

The female is a flower garden;
watered with love, grows with interest...

Yasemin's Desperation

CHAPTER
6

As promised, my boss came by the next morning and after breakfast we drove to the hospital with the children. In the meantime, Yasemin called. I told her that we were coming and that she shouldn't worry about her siblings as they were with me. She received us very frantically because she didn't want to stay in the hospital. She wanted to clarify where they could stay and what she should do as soon as possible to put her life in order. Her siblings would have to educate themselves, they would have to go back to school, but that wasn't possible while she was in the hospital.

She was consumed by fear that her siblings would remain as uneducated as she was, that they would be forced to drop out of school. You shouldn't miss a day from school.

Around eight o'clock both the doctors and the police entered the room. The doctors recommended that she stay in the hospital for inpatient psychological treatment. This did not suit Yasemin and she defended herself: "Not at this point in time, not even for one day. My siblings are not to be left behind, not to be taken out of their school. We can't stay here. We need to find a place to stay for ourselves. I have to build an orderly life for my siblings. They are far too young to be left alone."

Yasemin, who kept repeating these words, was still young herself. She tried to get up from her sickbed as she faced the painful realities of life she faced. She didn't want to waste time, so she tried to fix everything as quickly as possible.

Again we didn't have a chance to talk to Yasemin. I suspected that this conversation would only happen after Yasemin and her siblings were got through this horrible situation. So we drove back to the police station, where we were told that the three were taken to the women's shelter in Hanover. From there they received the help they needed. That was just fine with Yasemin, because she wanted to leave the city as quickly as possible and leave immediately: "I owe you a debt. We have weighed heavily on you with our worries. From now on I will continue my path with my siblings. You know where I am. When the police officers drop us off there, I'll call you. We'll keep in touch, I'll keep you posted, don't worry," she promised.

They hastily said goodbye to me as if they would never return. They got into the police car and drove away. This separation hurt me a lot. It was like we'd never see each other again. I was very sad, full of pain inside and I still couldn't talk to her. Yasemin was of legal age, old enough to build her own life, set sail and left the negative behind. She was looking for happiness and peace. She was gone...

Yasemin went as she came...

The past is erased, and all that remains is pain.

CHAPTER
7

My boss approached me affectionately: ""It was a very strenuous day, you better go home rest and get some sleep. You'll come when you're fit again." Since my brother was at work, I didn't want to be home alone at that moment. "No thanks, but I'm responsible for my job and I don't want to be alone now!", I confessed and so we drove to work together.

At the end of the day I was very sad and silent, physically and mentally exhausted from fatigue. After my shift, over dinner, I spoke to my brother about what we had experienced during the day. Suddenly Yasemin called and I got very excited. "We got a room. Please don't worry about us, we're fine. Tomorrow morning we will discuss all necessary procedures with the social workers. They will even take care of an apartment for us and find the right school for my siblings. They will get me a job, too," she babbled happily into the phone. When I heard this happy and hopeful voice, I was very relieved. A stone fell from my heart.

She really kept me informed of developments. "They didn't bring us to Hanover, they took us to Munster. They said you that for our safety," Yasemin explained. "Yasemin, don't leave me in the dark. Definitely let me know how it goes!" I asked her. After a short conversation, we ended the call.

Talking to her was of the utmost importance to me. My brother noticed my silence and spoke to me. He was always loving. His sensitive nature built me up and gave me strength. The story of Yasemin, which I had only heard a quarter of, and what I witnessed depressed me greatly. It made me feel like I was reliving my past. Yasemin was the first person to resemble my reflection. I certainly wasn't thinking of abandoning her. Yasemin called me every day. She always kept me informed of her progress and developments.

Her siblings were accepted at the school and they found a suitable apartment to move into at the end of the month. Yasemin stayed in the women's shelter until she moved. She was still in a hurry to look for a job, so she could not find peace and did not feel well. I also helped her to find a job on the Internet. I gave her the addresses of the jobs I had found that suited her. I even called them myself when needed. The more I could lighten their burden, the more peace filled me. As long as my Lord gave me this power.

I always wanted to be with Yasemin and her siblings and support them. Moving day was approaching. As a salon team, we wanted to surprise Yasemin with the most important housewares. Such as mattresses, duvets, pillows etc. We bought everything new and were with her the day she moved.

Their household appliances and furniture were organized by the women's shelter, which was funded by the state. Since Yasemin and her siblings were really in need of help, I was very happy that they got all the help they could need. I held forks, spoons, china plates, glasses, pots, etc. in excess. I put everything in boxes.

There was still no opportunity to talk to Yasemin alone. That fact ate me up inside. Since I had multiple jobs, I couldn't go to her every time I wanted, and Yasemin couldn't come to me because of her condition. Our calls were always short, we only discussed the important things on the phone. Yasemin finally found work. She recovered very quickly and stood tall in life. Her siblings were still at the top.

A heartbreaking day will surely be broken...

Yasemin's Desperation

CHAPTER
8

Next week Thursday was a public holiday. A long time ago, I had my vacation request approved so I could get a long weekend, which I desperately needed. I got permission from the lounge on Fridays and Saturdays and the restaurant on Sundays and Mondays. I wanted to visit Yasemin with my brother. Our phone calls grew longer and more intense every day. She spoke about all topics, about her pain, the sadness and the loneliness that she carried inside.

The day finally came, we visited Yasemin from Thursday to Sunday. The train journey took four hours. Yasemin was waiting for us with her siblings at the main train station. I was happy to finally see all three. We didn't have to walk far and finally arrived at her apartment. Yasemin had already prepared the breakfast table and brewed the tea. As soon as we sat down at the table, we talked about God and the world. Our laughter was an indication of how hungry and longing we were for joy and happiness. Yes, those of us at the breakfast table were hungry for joy and happiness!

My brother took all three into his heart, which made me very happy. The bond grew even stronger when the siblings started calling him uncle. Over time we became a real little family.

We talked about what we could do until Sunday and organized our days. I wanted Yasemin to rest, generate and do something good did for himself. So I had previously booked movie tickets online for the siblings to spend more time with them. Meanwhile, Yasemin should go to cosmetic skin care, massage, hairdressing and manicure. I had already booked the dates for her. It would be very good for your soul, both mentally and physically. This was my surprise for her and she was delighted. She started dancing and jumping like a little kid. She actually deserved more.

Everyone was talking at the same time, as if we feared being separated at any moment. We were always afraid that our meetings, which were far too short, could be the last. For the first few minutes we were chattering: "We do this and that, this goes like this." Even the tasting was great. It was the end of sad faces. The awful days of pain and frustration were over, it was like eternal happiness.

I never dreamed of making Yasemin talk and I never interrupted their conversations! I felt ready to listen if she wanted to talk about what had happened. The suggestion to talk had to come from her. Otherwise, I wouldn't have thought to bring up these issues so as not to upset, tire, or sadden them.

After breakfast, the kids took my brother to their room to show him their video games. We sat at the breakfast table, which we still hadn't covered, and comfortably drank our tea. In the meantime Yasemin had started smoking. "You don't even know how to pull it. Yasemin, it's best to stop before you can't stop," I admonished her.

"You're right!" she answered insightfully.

We started asking each other questions from everyday life. For example, whether she was satisfied with her working life, her new employer and her new environment.

"You were right, the barbers can't make a living from a salary. Like you, I also found an extra job!", said Yasemin. "What extra work? As what? Where? And where are your siblings at this time? What are they doing while you're gone?" I asked frantically. "They may be young, but they are the children who have been hit hard by life. Even at that age they can run the house without me for a week or two," she said simply.

It really was a painful truth of life. No child should have to bear this burden. They shouldn't have been under such responsibility. Again a picture of the harsh realities of life struck me.

As Yasemin addressed some issues, her chin stopped shaking. Before me now stood a hardened and stronger Yasemin. On the one hand I was very happy, on the other hand I was frankly scared. What had made Yasemin so hard overnight? What drove you to make this decision? What made her feel so callous from time to time?

This woman was no longer the Yasemin I knew. She made me think. It seemed like a turning point. While we were talking about all this, we had already cleared the breakfast table.

While Yasemin was on sick leave, she tried to get custody of her siblings. She actually got it by court order. This was the reward for their trust. Finally, her relatives could no longer take her siblings away from her. She had even been granted a ban on approaching her. Nobody knew where they lived, they were safe. Yasemin had been saved from the abyss of a great catastrophe. The nightmarish days were now behind her. However, I knew that her story would soon come out.

With great pride, Yasemin said, "Come on, let me show you the apartment and what else I've bought." We walked through the rooms, she showed me the new furniture and decorations that she had bought or received from the office. She was happy with her apartment and seemed to have found herself again. This situation made me very happy.

Since my brother was playing with the siblings in the children's room, I finally had the opportunity to talk to Yasemin. The questions asked at the breakfast table remained unanswered.

However, while making coffee, she started to talk: "A lot has changed in my life. I lost many things. I couldn't even be the leading lady of my life. I can stand up straight out of necessity, but I'm exhausted. I should be collapsing at my age, but I'm forcing myself to stand." She stood at the kitchen counter with her back to me, her attention focused on the coffee. Her sighing sentences hurt me. I understood her condition. Even if she didn't say anything, I understood very well what these feelings meant.

"I haven't told you everything about me. Everything was just too hectic, I couldn't keep up. To be honest, that day is still very much in my mind today," she admitted.

I looked at her sympathetically and whispered more than I spoke: "I didn't want to overwhelm you, let alone force you to talk about your fate and your pain. It wasn't time yet. Perhaps now is not the right time." Her jaw trembled, her eyes were focused and at times wandered far away. Yasemin was overwhelmed.

"I'd like to show you pictures from my past, but I don't have a single picture of my mother, father, or childhood. I even forgot my mother's face, I don't remember it. One word from my father always stuck in my mind. When I remember that word, I see his face in front of me. My father still hasn't left my memory!' she said, her emotion showing on her face.

"Why aren't there any pictures?" if I may ask. "My stepmother tore them all up!" she replied. 'There wasn't much, you know I told you. We sold everything we harvested from the vineyards, vegetable fields and orchards at the market. That's the only way we made a living. Our financial situation was not good."

"We are very similar, it wasn't much different for me when I was young. But thank God, there are worse fates. We should always be thankful. If we weren't strong, determined and ambitious, who knows what disasters we would have suffered. We are under God's protection as orphans. We managed to weather storms, resist the wind, no matter how many times the rain soaked us. We experienced hunger, slept outdoors and we are still standing."

We found ourselves in a deep conversation without knowing where the journey was going. But in front of me stood a hardened and very mature Yasemin. She had overcome her own problems, found the strength to endure the rest. Yasemin did not give up the resistance and survived.

Sometimes we were distracted by our coffee cups in hand, then we were again involved in intensive conversations. Suddenly she grabbed my arm while I was drinking my coffee. "When I was thirteen, they gave me to a 37-year-old man who lived near our village to be his wife. No matter how mature I seemed at that age because of the responsibilities I had taken on.

When I look back today, I see that I was indeed a child. I was never allowed to live my childhood. They didn't even give me a day of it."

With focused eyes, I stared at her as she narrated and placed my hand over hers, which was clutching my arm. She continued while I just listened: "I thought my father and stepmother made this decision together to give me to this man. I thought I was mature, but I really didn't understand what was going on. One day, after a few weeks had passed, my stepmother was in a hurry and urged me, "Put on your dress, look good. Get ready, we're going. Hurry up!" I quickly stopped doing the housework, got ready and thought, "How nice, we're going for a ride." They took me with them for the first time. My stepmother's scolding didn't move me, I began to be happy. It didn't take long, I had maybe five minutes to dress then she urged: "Come on, hurry up! Why are you dallying?" I couldn't look in the mirror because of her rush. So I rushed out of my room and ran to the door. My stepmother snapped at me, "You haven't even combed your hair yet. I hope they don't change their minds." She threw open the door and pulled me outside by my hair.

I couldn't disagree with my stepmother, who insulted me with thousands of hurtful words on the way. Frantically she brought me to the main street. A car was parked on the side of the road and an old man got out. He whispered mysteriously to my stepmother. "Who are these people? Where is my father? Why didn't he come?' I thought, but couldn't find any answers.

I didn't get an answer to my questions, which at some point I began to ask out loud and kept repeating. She just put me in the car. "Come on, get in. I'll come now too," she promised. I watched my stepmother and never took my eyes off her for a moment. She kept talking to this man outside, my fear growing every second. A woman and another man were in the car. The older lady kept mumbling and distracting me, "Is this our young bride?" My stepmother and this man were discussing some things that I found strange.

It was the dowry she accepted.

The old man got back in the car so I sat in the middle. I thought my stepmother would get in too, but the driver started the car and drove off. "My stepmother would come, too," I told myself, horrified. "We're going home, she's coming in the evening," said the old man. Who were the people in the car? I didn't know any of them from the surrounding villages, I had never seen this car in the neighborhood either.

Eventually we stopped in a village. "We're here," the man informed me. "They're not from here, they're just taking me somewhere, but where?" I thought. The older woman asked me, "Tell me, little girl, what's your name? How old are you?" I answered her questions truthfully. "Your name is beautiful, but your fate is filled with bad luck. The girl is so young," she said to the older man who was her husband.

Only then did I understand that they were taking me to the house of the man I considered an uncle. So my stepmother wanted me to get ready and dress well. I started to cry because I still didn't know what was going on or what that meant.

We stopped in front of a three storey house that belonged to the man I called Uncle. "We're here, get out!" he said. The old man and the elderly woman abandoned me, even though they escorted us into the house, I felt alone. Thousands of questions in my brain were starting to find answers one by one. My stepmother had sold me to this man by accepting my dowry."

While Yasemin was telling this, she cried. Her chin was trembling and her eyes were filled with tears. I got up and brought her a handkerchief, then I asked my brother: "Keep looking after the children, I will speak to Yasemin." Then I went back to Yasemin. This time she was very determined, she wanted to talk. She wanted to get rid of her inner burden, to get rid of all the problems that were nagging at her.

I wanted to listen to her without asking questions and let her know that I would always support her. Still tearful, Yasemin relived what she said with every tear. I didn't want to hug her now and silence her or stop her from crying. It was time to let it all out. You're in good hands, I'm with you, I tried to convey with my body language and stretched out my hands to her. Yasemin, feeling that sincerity and trust, said, "I'm in safe hands, thank God!"

From now on I could have guessed what had happened to her, but I preferred to let Yasemin talk without interrupting her until she said, "Stop! Stop!" STOP" shouted. More often than not, events were worse, more catastrophic, and heartbreaking than anticipated. So I wanted to put my guesses aside and just listen to her. I put a glass of cold water next to the empty coffee cups.

Yasemin was tired of crying, but relieved at the same time. She sighed deeply after taking a few sips of water. Yasemin, determined to pick up where she left off, continued: »If you don't want to, we don't need to delve deeper into the subject. I'm so confused I don't even know what to tell. You know not everyone can be spoken to, not everyone can be trusted. Ever since I was a child, the chaos of people has left a scar on my heart. I don't want to confuse you, but I want to pick up where I left off."

I nodded to her encouragingly and Yasemin picked up the thread again: "I can still hear how surprised and amazed everyone present whispered when we entered the house with the old woman: "She is still a child!" I have a few things forgotten, it's like they've been erased from my memory, but I remember that day as clearly as if it were yesterday.

In my shy and fearful state, I looked at everyone. Questions swirled in my head like, "Where was my father? Why did my stepmother put me in the car?" "Did you kidnap me?" I almost screamed. I had to know.

"No, we have not! Your stepmother accepted our dowry," explained the person's brother, whom I took to be a 37-year-old uncle. The old woman who brought me here showed by her demeanor that she was very optimistic and compassionate. I was supposed to get up and set the table, then she said, "Don't say that, son, it's not our girl's fault. She's just a kid."

I didn't even dare to go to the toilet for fear. I couldn't do this at home because my stepmother was in a hurry. The old woman had entered the kitchen. It was only then that I dared to mention: "I really need to go to the toilet."

"Don't run, you're going to get in trouble. I'll help you get out of here," she promised, taking me to the bathroom. She waited outside the door until I was done.

I couldn't hold back my tears and ran out of the bathroom crying. I was getting hysterical and loudly emphasizing my questions: "What's going on here? Tell me why did you bring me here? I have to go home. Does my father know I'm here?'

"Your stepmother sold you!" his brother revealed to me. "Will you have such a cheeky tongue from day one? You must be chastised as a sapling at a young age." He came to me in a rage and hit me with all his might. I covered my face with my hands and hit the ground. It was only this old woman who helped me: "Don't! She's just a kid! She doesn't know what happened, keep your hands off her. If your brother comes, you'll be in trouble."

Everyone looked at me, I ran to the bathroom without looking at anyone and cried. I locked up behind me. There was a loud knock at the door. I didn't understand what was going on. "Open the door, open the door!" someone yelled. I was scared and cried even more.

As the pounding on the door continued, I noticed more and more voices mingling. More people had come into the house. "Will they all come to me now?" a voice in my head screamed in panic.

Suddenly it got quiet. After a while, the old woman's words came muffled through the door: "Hey little one, open the door, don't be afraid! I'm here, they took him away from the house." I felt relieved, trusting the old woman. Despite my fear, I slowly opened the door and as promised, she stood alone in front of me.

"Come to me, I'll tell you what I know and what you need to know," she said softly to me. Only I couldn't calm down. 'Where did they go, will he come back? Does he live in this house?" I sobbed.

"He lives downstairs!" she confessed. We sat on the bed and she explained it to me one by one. From time to time I would interrupt them and ask questions that came to my mind in surprise and fear. "I know him from the weekly market, I haven't even spoken to him. I'm only 13 years old. He came every now and then and bought a lot from us, but I'm not sure if that's the person I call uncle?"

"Little one, didn't you see him when he came to your house?" she asked.

"No! My stepmother wouldn't let me out of the room. I didn't even see him," I wailed.

The older woman replied, "Oh, your stepmother looks like a snake! Everything came from her side. She also got your gift as a bridal gift. Your father doesn't know you're here. They kidnapped you here."

"We have to do something, please save me from here," I begged the old woman through sobs. "Give me a moment to think. How can we make it without taking damage? Let me have a talk with my husband," she pleaded.

Suddenly someone came into the house and I started shaking. My curiosity was satisfied. Now I knew what was going on.

A loud voice called, "Where are you?"

As we waited for the new arrivals, I begged the older woman, "Please do something! Go to the police, tell them I was kidnapped. Do it, please, please... help me!"

The front door opened. Three women and four men stood in front of the door. "Come in!" said a voice from the next room. Then the crowd came in and we walked over to them. We were all sitting somewhere in the spare room, but I kept my head down. I couldn't look into the faces of those who were so bad. An old man in the room got nervous and snapped at me, "Get up, what are you sitting on? Give her proper clothing that covers her body, or we'll soon lose honor. As freely as she is dressed, she puts horns on my son. She has already turned my younger son's head. Stand up!"

I screamed in great shock. "Do you know what you're even saying?" I jumped out of my seat and just kept going, "This is too much, it was you who did this evil to me. You kidnapped me, I want to go home!" He walked up to me, kicked and hit me, insulted and abused me verbally. Again it was only thanks to the old woman that nothing worse happened and he let go of me. This couldn't be my destiny. I didn't want to experience this tyranny. The women who were visiting said: "Be quiet girls, shame on you! If you're like that on day one, who knows what socks you'll knit next."

I was dragged and pushed upstairs, but this time I didn't cry. This house that I was kidnapped into at the age of thirteen only made me stronger with the unjust words and beatings.

The women who brought me upstairs were my sisters-in-law from now on. They said, "We're your sisters-in-law, don't contradict us." But not everyone was like that. One of the three women standing in front of me was the wife of the man I was to marry. I was to become his second wife when I was 13 years old. The world collapsed on me, I suffered one of the worst hits in life. She witnessed every moment. Although she was even more angry than I was, she said nothing. I hadn't even heard her voice. We hadn't had a chance to talk because of the other two women. Our eyes met and revealed what we had been through. The woman, his first wife, was only 24 years old. She was young, very innocent and sad.

Yasemin had finished her last sentence. She was deep in her nightmares. Her gaze focused on one point. I patted her back with one hand to comfort her, then got up and carried our empty coffee cups into the kitchen. Yasemin had a great nightmare, as well as disasters, fear, torture and …

We had talked for almost two hours. Yasemin got up too, followed me into the kitchen, hugged me and breathed: "Nice to have you. I'm glad you're here!"

It was necessary for me to approach her gently and be very sensitive to her. It should open step by step. Understanding and tolerance were now in the foreground.

Never give up! Hope;
It's man's only refuge, remember.

CHAPTER
9

While we were talking, my brother took the children to the ice cream shop. We called him and asked, "How are you? Where are you? What are you doing?" He answered curtly, "We're coming home." So we waited for her in the living room, and I told Yasemin, "I checked online, there's a beautiful riverside park near your house with restaurants and cafeterias. What do you say, when the kids come home, should we all go together? The fresh air would be very good for us, we can eat in the restaurant and come home relaxed after a walk.

Yasemin agreed enthusiastically: "That would be great, the park isn't far from here, that's true. Let me get the kids' clothes ready and I'll change quickly."

The kids came and we went out as discussed. They talked about the school, about the lessons and how they dealt with their classmates. Along the way we were cheerful and the conversation was refreshing. We ate at a great restaurant, then went for a long walk before finding our way home. After playing all sorts of brain games, several hours had passed and the children were yawning. So they got ready to sleep and went to bed. My brother also said goodbye and lay down. We women cleaned up the apartment, then we made ourselves comfortable on the sofa.

With the same excitement, Yasemin began to narrate the continuation of her life: "Those other two women I told you about gave me a shawl to cover my hair like a shalwar. They insisted that I wear them. Because they just thought, "I would seduce their husbands with the clothes I wore." I don't understand these people. Didn't these people notice the plight I was in? There were no more words for it. They did me so much injustice and slandered me. I was a child, they were women who already had children of their own. "How can a woman do such tyranny to another woman?"

The woman whose husband I was to marry remained silent. She sat on the bed like a disconsolate angel and appeared to be in shock, but didn't intervene. Why did she endure the injustice done to her? I didn't know anything about her yet. After enough insults, she suddenly got up from her bed and said, "Okay, that's enough! You don't even want to stop. I'm getting tired of your tyranny. Leave us alone now. Go down, we'll be right behind you."

It was the first time she spoke and I was glad that she spoke. In fact the women went down and we were both alone. I felt that she was a good person. "I'm very sorry about what happened to you. You're still so small. You are a child, I was shocked to see you. What kind of humanity is that? Is there no more grace or conscience in this world? As if what they have already done to you is not enough, they put you down. Your father is not to blame. The snake, your stepmother, my father-in-law and my mother-in-law are the culprits," admitted the poor woman, who began cursing herself for accepting her fate.

"None of us knows what's going to happen now. Do they even know what a mess they've done to us?" I wailed.

The name of the woman who suddenly dropped and cried was Leyla. She told me she couldn't have children. The only reason they brought me here was to continue their family tree. Her name would live on for generations. In my opinion, her name should be erased from the origin of the generation!

"Are you already on your period?" Leyla asked shyly. Bowing my head, I answered hesitantly and embarrassed, "Yes, why do you ask?"

"Since they brought you here in such a hurry, I'm sure they'll put you in my husband's bed soon. Your bleeding means you can have children and they want children from you!" she revealed to me and I was shocked. I didn't understand the word sexuality because I didn't know what it meant. I only understood it after she told me that they wanted to have children by me.

"Please help me, please help me to escape," I begged her.'"It's a crime, I call him uncle, he used to come to the weekly market to buy from us. Although I'm not at all sure myself that it really is him."

"Can't do anything, he won't even let me go to the neighbors! What can I do? I'm a victim of my own fate," Leyla said bitterly. She hugged me and started crying.

When I asked, "Will they only have a baby if I'm bleeding?" I got some hope because she replied, "Exactly, only then." So I asked them to lie for me and tell them I hadn't gotten my period yet. That's how I bought time. "I never thought that you were so small that you had such a clever head. I'll try," Leyla promised. "You stay up here and I'll go down to my mother-in-law's. I'll tell her you're not bleeding yet and they should wait until you are. It'll buy us time before we get out of here." She left me and walked away.

My future mother-in-law and Leyla came up two minutes later. "Hey little chick, your stepmom said you already had your period!" the vixen said harshly, resting a hand on her waist as if expecting an explanation. I lowered my head and whispered:

"No, not yet." In truth, I remembered that moment very well.

"Oh, what happened to us? Oh, sir, if I had known, I would have waited," the fox wailed, sitting on the bed and beginning to beat her knees in desperation. She keeps repeating, "Oh my lord!"

I was very grateful to Layla! Luckily she had told me about the bleeding. I still kept my head down. Leyla stood in the room and rubbed her hands, she knew that the vixen still had something devious in mind and she was right, she said it out loud: "Let's leave her alone for the weekend, then we'll take her to the gynecologist. Maybe there's something he can do to make the bleeding start sooner."

We were amazed. This woman was a real bitch! How could a woman do something so bad to a girl, her fellow man? Was there no conscience, no mercy or compassion in her? I didn't understand how a woman could be so cruel to a woman?

The fox was furious and snapped at us, "Come on, everyone's hungry. You don't have to wait for your troubles to end. Go downstairs and prepare the meals. Leyla, show her where everything is." All eyes were on me, everyone followed me with their gaze, from small to large. This time I wore a scarf over my hair and a shalwar. I had never been covered.

I worked at a hairdresser for three years. I started when I was ten years old. I had to use my wits and do whatever it took to get rid of this man. That required patience. Thanks to Leyla, I had gained a few days to look for a way out and plan my escape. I had to find a way out. Crying didn't help. I had to be careful with every word I said. I once chose the good from the bad, Leyla. Thanks very much! She had helped me a lot, although she wasn't aware of it. I wish I could help her too, but I was like a helpless moth.

While I was preparing the meals with Leyla, the other two women entered the kitchen. "As we see, you are already united, Leyla!," they said viciously. "How can you accept her right away when she's been wagging her butt in front of our men from day one?"

Leyla was annoyed by such words. "Get out! It's none of your business. Go mind your own business," Leyla kicked them out. Even though the kitchen was too small for so many people, they still stayed where they were.

"Please ignore her. Don't let the words get to you," Leyla asked me desperately and gently stroked my head. The woman with her rude mouth, bad morals and mentality said, "Okay, we're going out. Not your mouth, but your hands should work, we're hungry."

"My God! My God!" she begged the Lord and prayed quietly: "Save us from this calamity and from this need." In order to remain calm, I said softly every time: "Amin!".

We prepared lunch for almost 30 people. The pots were huge, like for a wedding dinner. I later realized that every meal was so sumptuous it was nothing special. As time went by, more and more people came. Everyone wanted to see me, they looked me up and down. Aunts, sisters, husbands and old uncles, amazed to see me, covered their mouths with their hands. I felt very uncomfortable like a hunted gazelle. I was distressed and disgusted by those who walked into the kitchen just to look at me. I felt like I was in the slave market.

If I had a mother or an older brother, would none of this have happened to me. Yasemin audibly breathed in and out deeply again and again. She crossed her legs in silence, took the ashtray and put it on the cushion. She leaned back against the seat and watched the white smoke from her cigarette. She went deep into her thoughts in her own way. In that moment, she was transported back to her life eight years ago. She was reliving that nightmarish time again.

I said nothing, I was silent. After each puff she stared at the smoke, lost in the depths of her soul. Her body was with me, her spirit far away. From time to time the cigarette sat in the ashtray, then she would reach out and watch her. It was like saying, "What did those hands see? What have these hands endured? What went through those hands?" Yasemin didn't even notice her silence. She pictured the scenes she told me like a movie, like the credits of her past. It was now 12:45 a.m. and Yasemin was tired. Her narratives were no longer fluent. Her breaks increased. But she wanted to talk, to free herself by explaining her life situation at all costs. She stubbed out her cigarette and continued where she left off.

Cheers erupted in the house. As if there was a wedding to celebrate. It was full. There were people in every room. In the garden the women lit a fire, even a lamb was speared and roasted over the fire. I didn't want to raise my head, didn't want to see or recognize anyone. I avoided eye contact with the bad guy. I concentrated on cooking with Leyla.

The fox rushed in and scolded, "Who are these meals supposed to be enough for? The house is full of people." She pushed Leyla and I aside, then chided us, "Move your hands faster."

Much food had already been prepared. At least six to seven different dishes, with the lamb turning over the fire outside. What I experienced back then was a nightmare. My psyche suffered and this woman thought nothing had happened. I was surprised. My thoughts went to my father. He didn't know

I was here and that my stepmother had sold me. While trying to somehow reach him to get out of here as quickly as possible, I became unable to move due to the stress. I used to think, "If Leyla can't even go to the neighbor's, how can I get out of here before something happens to me?" I shouldn't have distracted myself from what I could do with these pessimistic and cowardly thoughts. I had to find a solution and escape from there without taking any damage.

Everyone was gathered in the house. Only the man I was supposed to marry was probably not there. Maybe he was there and I hadn't seen him? Because I was still in the kitchen to prepare the food. The women who came in to set the table caused chaos and panic. My thoughts were with father. It was quite late, everyone had eaten and the tables were being cleared. Leyla and I couldn't eat a spoonful. "Okay, sit down and eat something too," nobody said to us. Leyla was very depressed, she submitted to everything. Was that my destiny too? Should I end up like Leyla?

I was desperate, but also determined. No, this was not my destiny." The crowd dispersed. Only family members remained in the house and went to their own apartments. The man who was promised to me was still not there. I wonder if this situation was forced upon him as well? Did he want to show that he objected by not being present? I knew nothing.

The first hits, kicks, humiliations I received had frightened me and made me tremble.

Yasemin, who was lighting another cigarette, just wanted to get back into her thoughts, but I wouldn't let her. "You were very strong today and very energetic. I congratulate you! It takes a lot of strength and time to open up. I think we shouldn't exaggerate. We still have a few days to talk. Tomorrow we have to get up with the children. Let's smoke our last cigarette and go to bed. What do you say to that?" I asked, my eyes almost half-closed. "That's a very good idea, I'm pretty tired," she admitted. Relieved, she stood up and said: "It felt good to talk to you and to pour out my heart. I haven't talked about these topics in years. I've always repressed it, eaten it all up inside me. Now I feel free as a bird."

I was very happy to see her like this. But also quite tired, because I wasn't used to staying up late at night. Thanks to the adrenaline, I was still standing at this late hour. We were both ready for bed and I fell asleep as soon as I lay down. In the morning the children prepared the breakfast table for us. My brother had a childhood similar to that of his siblings. He too was raised in the hands of his older sister. So there was an extraordinary bond between the three, despite their age difference.

Yasemin woke up happy. Their cheerful mood surprised and delighted us. When Yasemin entered the kitchen, she was happy about the breakfast and said: "Oh, I feel twenty kilos lighter, good morning!" We had a nice chat, and Yasemin dived back into the dream world with a slight smile. Then she suddenly grabbed my arm with her hand. "You have the gift of writing. When I read your lyrics and poems, they touch my heart. What do you say, would you write my life down?" she asked me. Excited and full of hope, she waited for my answer. Her eyes lit up, how could I say no to her? I gave her a small smile and said, "If you want, I'll be happy to write down your life story."

"Hooray!" Yasemin roared, leaping up from her seat and dancing with joy. She hugged me and kissed my head as I danced. Her joy was contagious, the children got up and danced enthusiastically. It was the first time I saw her happy and enthusiastic. It was a very good feeling of happiness that Yasemin and her siblings had earned since childhood. After the emotional outburst, she turned the music down, then sat down at the table. She tried to suppress her excitement by saying, "I couldn't control my emotion, but it felt good." As we cleared the table together after dinner, she asked, "But how do we do that? You wouldn't mention my name, would you? We find another name for me and my siblings. I'm going to be the leading lady of my life for the first time." "Yasemin, it's not as easy as you think. Of course I would like to write your life story, but there are also legal aspects that we have to consider. The person who allows me to write their life down not only has to reveal their real life but also notarize it. Since it's public, it has to be proven why her name was changed." Yasemin immediately brought her files, which she had already prepared for the project, to me. "Look, I have proof, my siblings and I can change our names for our own safety."

"I saw your story, I saw what there was to see. You don't have to show me that evidence. We have to present them legally," I told her. Yasemin was very eager. I didn't see the negative sides either, but why should we give ourselves unnecessary headaches now. If we did it right from the start, was there no trouble? The whole apartment showed that Yasemin was a book lover. There were books everywhere on the windowsill, on the shelves, simply spread throughout the house. She was so in love with reading. She seemed to devour the books as she read. The best present for her was a book.

"It is Friday! Our vacation is coming to an end. Who knows when we can get back together? What are you saying? Shall we go to the notary? Shall we have our book project notarized?" she repeated her questions happily. Her eyes radiated hope. She wanted to share her life, which was full of pain, with others and announce it to the world. "Of course you thought well, why not. Let's not put off our book project for another time. Our vacation is the best opportunity. Who knows when we can meet again?' I agreed. She was happy... She was very happy... so was I, for I enjoyed the same happiness as her. At that moment, Yasemin radiated hope in every respect. So agreed we made an online appointment with the next notary for the same day and received our first approval.

Back home, Yasemin remembered: "I forgot to buy something. Who wants to come with me?" So she went shopping with my brother Murat and her brother Suat. Until they came back I was able to spend some time with their sister Kiraz. In the kitchen, she took out the ingredients for the yeast dough and placed them one by one in a bowl. I was surprised to see that she could do this on her own. "What do you do with these ingredients?" I asked curiously. "I'll knead the dough, let it rise until it ferments. I want to make a pastry today,' she replied. I started laughing in surprise.

Unbelievable! For her age, she was great at giving answers. Anyone would understand my surprise if they could see her going into the kitchen, taking out the ingredients, putting them into the bowl one by one, and kneading the dough with her tiny hands. Across from me was an 8-year-old girl. She was very mature for her age. This little girl's name is Kiraz. Now I ask you: "Who of you in Germany knows an eight-year-old girl like Kiraz, who can knead yeast dough on her own?

With her tiny hands, she left out no ingredients and formed a perfect, beautiful dough? Have you seen an eight-year-old do it on her own? I don't think so! On the one hand I want you to see it, on the other I don't. It's an image that will make you say "superb," but at the same time, it's an image of life's painful realities.

Everyone lives their own destiny. She was a little girl who kneaded the dough with her tiny hands. Although I'd offered to give her a hand, I was amazed when she said, "No, you can sit down, I'll make coffee for you, you can rest." Kiraz couldn't be a child, at least up to that day she had not experienced a childhood and was forced to master life due to the circumstances. While Kiraz kneaded the dough, I made hot cocoa for her and coffee for myself. As she covered the dough, she explained, "It will be fermented in an hour, then we can bake it." Again, she made me laugh with that phrase, but this time she joined me. She was quite successful in school, she was a smart, intelligent and decent girl who loved to read.

We were just having our coffee and cocoa when the others got home. Yasemin stood in front of me with a bag in her hand and said: "I hope you like my gift? Please take it!" Suddenly I was very excited and accepted the bag she handed me. Yasemin had a present for me. "Don't be shy... Please open up, I hope this is the first step towards your successful book project," she said. My heart was beating faster, my hands were shaking and I excitedly opened the package. Yasemin's gift was a tape recorder with ten small cassettes. I gratefully hugged Yasemin with shining eyes. She really managed to surprise me.

"I thought it would be easier this way. We'll pick up from where we left off last night. What do you say?" she asked me. That was a stupid question, of course I thought the idea was great. Yasemin was like a flower about to wither. They hadn't managed to tear out their root. Yasemin rebelled, made himself heard. She resisted, screaming with every fiber of her body: "This is not my destiny, this is not my destiny, I became a victim! Why shouldn't I stand up and object?" Well done, Yasemin… Yasemin's scream was just one of thousands. A character who wanted her voice to be heard.

For her security, she used a pseudonym. She wanted to live properly, she and her siblings. Maybe those with the same mentality will wake up. Perhaps those who are victims gain strength with their stories. Yasemin had more to tell me than I thought. She filled one volume after the other with her life story. She spoke as if she were writing a letter. "I haven't told you an eighth of what I've been through," everything said. She was now ready to speak. Yasemin tried to escape from her nightmare with speeches.

"Shall we drop our other plans this lunchtime and go to the park so the kids can have fun? Your siblings couldn't be children. While you work, they take care of the housework, even cook. If necessary, they also go shopping. You are 21 years old and have become the man of the house. Let's all be children today, let's live our childhood, which we didn't live, which unfortunately we weren't allowed to live a day," I begged her. Yasemin looked at my confused face. "You're right," she agreed. When she was young, she had three jobs to support herself. She carried a heavy burden on her shoulders. Her siblings tried to support her as much as possible and for that she was very grateful. Little Kiraz came to us and informed us: "My dough is already fermented. It doesn't take much time to prepare the filling and finish the pastries." Not leaving Kiraz alone in the kitchen, we began our preparations.

When we were done we visited the park which had amazing views. There were nice sidewalks and small shops, boutiques, restaurants and cafeterias along the river. There was even a small beach. The children took their bathing suits with them. We settled in a suitable place and prepared the picnic with fruits, pastries, salads and drinks. Short, sweet conversations took place between us. The walls between Yasemin and us had been torn down. She even smiled at her painful memories from time to time, as if she were breaking down the barriers that lay ahead.

After spending almost four hours in the park, we headed home. Everyone felt more comfortable and calmer than the day before. A touch of happiness and joy wafted around us. Yasemin couldn't stand it any longer, so she spoke to me: "I've talked to my siblings, they'll give us a little rest. What do you say, let's start our first recording?", "If you want, of course!" I agreed. Of course I wanted to, but I didn't force her. I gave her time to breathe. "I'm ready, I'll listen to you, we can start," I offered. Over the years, Yasemin has faced social pressures that have had a negative impact on her. Many of us are victims of this oppression. Even when she lived her life of her own free will, there was this pressure, a small example was: "What does a stranger or neighbor say or think about me?" The decisions of those around us guided our private lives. Yasemin became a victim of this social pressure because she wasn't allowed to make decisions about her own life.

Although the weather was good, Yasemin could not sit and speak on the balcony as she was still suffering from the influence of the pressure. "What if my neighbors hear what I'm talking about? What will they think of me? It's not my fault what happened to me," she thought aloud.

"It's easy to say that everyone controls their own destiny, but hard to put into practice. You must not allow the thoughts, otherwise you will always be a victim of social oppression.

Don't let anyone force you into something you don't want. Nobody tells you that you have to talk on the balcony. You decide everything for yourself. Nobody has the right to make decisions about your privacy. Please keep this in mind throughout your life. You have siblings, you've been taking care of them for years. Nobody comes up to you and asks how you're doing. You are your own master now. Take care of your siblings and their freedom as you take care of yours.

"No more restrictions, you are no longer victims of social oppression," I encouraged Yasemin. Yasemin didn't interrupt me and listened to me from start to finish. "You're right… I'll teach my siblings the same way, but as far as I'm concerned, it's a bit difficult to stick to. I hope I can get over this feeling and this situation quickly," she confessed to me. This was not only true for Yasemin, but for thousands of people like her. I had expressed a universal and social problem. It wasn't a lie either…

The tea was ready, our hazelnuts and peanuts were on the table along with the tape recorder. Yasemin eagerly awaited our conversation. I could feel her excitement all over my body. She was my heroine. After Yasemin had carried out the first attempts and deleted them, she said: "We can start now."

A woman forcibly touched,
Cannot Be Silenced!

CHAPTER
10

The crowd was scattered, with only family members staying at home. They cleaned up and then got ready for bed. I cried again and thought of my father. What had they told him? Leyla said desperately, "Your father didn't know you were brought here."

What will he think now that I am? That thought made me very sad. I want to add and underline that I didn't know their names, they didn't get the honor, they were evil. I called Leyla's mother-in-law vixen, although after a while she also became my mother-in-law. A mother cannot be strict and cruel, she should not be! Now you know why I couldn't call her mother-in-law.

"Don't worry, I'll protect you as best I can," Leyla soothed me. It was a relief for me, I trusted her. "Ferhat should have been here by now. When he comes, we will tell him everything. Maybe he's just as much a victim as we are. We don't know, we'll both talk to him when he comes,' she promised me. The name of the man I addressed as uncle was Ferhat. It was the first time I learned his name. Wasn't that strange? It was approaching to 1:00 a.m. I was exhausted, very tired, but they still didn't want me to leave to let.

In front of the front door of the garden, a loud noise startled us. I got scared and hid behind Leyla. She held me like she was protecting me with one hand. The loud noise stayed for a while. This time the voice of a man who suddenly started yelling and laughing at the same time echoed throughout the house. Family members who had gone to their homes came back to us. Everyone asked the same thing: "What's going on?" The men went out to investigate.

It was Uncle Ferhat coming home drunk. I was very shocked. It was the first time I saw a drunk. He stank from the drink, I was disgusted. Why did you get drunk until you lost your mind?

I was still watching the horrifying scene from afar, staying hidden behind Leyla. Leyla was also very worried, she literally panicked and accused everyone: "You lit the fire in my family." She ran to her apartment on the upper floor, crying, and I was left alone. Should I chase after Leyla? I was terrified, wide-eyed, body shaking, watching what happened next. They beat me again, it was my fault. Suddenly this vixen yelled at me: "What are you standing there, hurry up! You've caused such problems from day one."

I was surprised. Was it I who brought them this trouble? I didn't come voluntarily. My stepmother had sold me when I was 13 years old child. I had a lot of responsibilities, worked, looked after the house and my siblings from morning to night, prepared the food, worked in the fields or gardens, sold our goods in the market and, on top of that, worked in the barber shop... But I was still a child. I wasn't responsible for this nightmare...

Half nervous, half angry, tired and exhausted, I stood in the room without raising any objections. Suddenly Leyla came back crying, grabbed my arm and said, "You're coming with me, I can't leave you with them."

Leyla didn't let go of me that night. Her father-in-law, mother-in-law and my sisters-in-law came to the apartment. They beat Leyla very badly because she protected me. While trying to shield them with my tiny body, I was also hit. "It all happened because of you, whatever happened to us happened because of you. We're going to die out because of you and we won't be able to continue the generation," they accused Leyla, beating her more and more. Leyla didn't resist, it wasn't her fault. Why was this family like this?

I didn't know this violence, I was never hit by my mother or my father. It wasn't until my stepmother came into the house that the beatings started. She pushed, humiliated me and threw the worst words at me, sometimes more painful than the bruises, bumps and strains. Violent people were weak, characterless and had a sick psyche. I hated them all.

Poor Leyla got beaten black and blue. The two sisters-in-law were also present and watched what was happening to Leyla without showing any emotion. What conscience and humanity did they carry within them? I still had trouble understanding it to this day!

At that moment, Uncle Ferhat entered the apartment in a drunken state, rocking menacingly. "Hi! Who's beating my wife here in my apartment?" he yelled, attacking the others. I repeat the name, it was Ferhat ... The uncle chased them all out of his apartment, and the three of us were left behind. I was shy and looking for a place to hide. They were both in very bad shape. Leyla was bleeding from her nose and her lips were split. Uncle Ferhat was drunk and fell into bed with his clothes on. Maybe he wasn't himself because he was drinking, but when he saved Leyla from the thugs, I thought he was a compassionate and conscientious person.

I had to help Leyla but I was too shy. She slowly got up off the floor and sat on her bed, crying. She covered her face with her hands. I drew Leyla's attention to me, made her sign that she should come to me. It was very difficult for her to get up. I quickly walked over to her, grabbed her arm to support her, then we stumbled onto the bathroom together. Leyla was still crying and I washed her face.

What situation did these people put the beautiful Leyla in? As I cursed them all, she suddenly turned to me. "Don't swear! God hears everything! Don't swear, it doesn't suit your innocent mouth. Don't get used to it at such a young age," she admonished me.

Since that day I had never cursed until today. Leyla, who always thought of me first, brought me to an empty room. "Come on, sleep here tonight. Take the keys please lock your door at night. We should take our precautions," she said. I thanked Leyla and locked the door from the inside. At that moment I felt safe, even though I was still scared. But being able to lock that door made me feel safe and secure.

I lay down exhausted and tried to keep my eyes open. Just in case someone showed up at the door and tried to get in with a spare key. I really tried. If I didn't sleep, I wouldn't be strong tomorrow. Who knew what awaited me? Today I was with Leyla, who protected me. What about tomorrow? So it wasn't long before I fell asleep.

The mosque was very close to here. The Imam's call to prayer woke me up. I hadn't slept much, but it was better than not at all. So I got up from my sleeping place and sat down on the sofa. When I moved, my whole body ached from the beating, yesterday I didn't even realize it because I was so excited.

I heard pots and spoons clattering in the kitchen. A person walked back and forth. I really needed to go to the bathroom, if I swept past I would be noticed. It could only be Leyla. I silently went to the bathroom, washed my hands and my face, which was marked by my distress. When I was done, I stepped out and was startled to find Uncle Ferhat standing in front of me. I was scared, hadn't expected him. He looked at me and asked me: "Come, sit down at the table, let's talk a little."

I followed him, shaky and afraid, my voice shaking, I could only stammer, "Well mm... Well..." Where was Leyla? She should have been with us. "Won't there be any secrets between the two of us?" he growled with a dirty grin.

What happened now? My fear grew. "I'm going back into the room. Let's talk later, Uncle Ferhat," I squeaked, but he grabbed my arm roughly. "Let's talk now!" he commanded.

Even though he noticed my fear, he continued to behave in such a bossy manner. This family has no common sense, I thought and started to cry.

Uncle Ferhat snapped at me, "I can't stand the crying, stop it." For calling him uncle, he grabbed my chin angrily. With his big hands he pulled me towards him and said to my face: "I'm not your uncle, you're my wife, accept that, get used to the situation."

Leyla's promising words made me think that I could escape from here. So in my mind I didn't notice the presence of a wild animal instead of a human. "Sit down now!" Uncle Ferhat instructed firmly and firmly. In order not to cause any further problems, I obeyed him. But I didn't stop crying. "Stop crying, now is not the time," he kept repeating, but my tears just flowed down my face. I couldn't hold her back.

I watched him out of the corner of my eye, head down. He still wasn't sober. How could I know that he drank until morning! Uncle Ferhat continued to drink even at the breakfast table. He put the bottle on the table and filled his glass half with alcohol and half with water. Today I know that drink was raki. He got up, took a second glass from the shelf above the kitchen counter, placed it in front of me and filled it up.

"Drink, you'll loosen up. Your fear will go away and your excitement will subside. Let's talk comfortably,' he prompted. I protested vigorously, "No, I don't drink, I don't want to drink." Although I was appalled, he kept pouring. He repeatedly said: "Drink!" How many times have I said that I don't want to drink, but in vain. I started crying because I wanted to go home. "Take me home," I begged. "What did you tell my father? My father doesn't know I'm here. He will wonder where I am?"

My voice grew louder and louder as I sensed the danger. My goal was to wake up the household. I figured if I got louder it would do some good. "Do not Cry! Don't yell!" he yelled at me, trying to shut me up. With tears my voice got louder, I wanted to wake Leyla.

A short time later, Leyla came running out of her room in a hurry. "What's going on here?" she asked angrily. "Ferhat, please don't touch the girl. She is just a child. You're drunk. You'll regret it when you're sober. You will not be able to look at yourself in the mirror. You'll be ashamed of what you've done."

"Stop talking, go to your room. How do you know how I'll feel? Shut the door, don't disturb me," he snapped at her. In fact, she went to her room without further objection, cowardly and intimidated.

Uncle Ferhat filled his glass again and drank it down in one gulp, then looked at me with small eyes. He came up behind me, put his hands on my shoulders and started stroking me. I was disgusted and pushed his hands away. I tried to get up from my seat. But he pushed me down.

"Okay, let's talk whatever you want to talk about, Uncle Ferhat! But please don't touch me, don't be bad to me,' I begged him, crying.

"Look, we understand each other," he said with a slight, devious smile. He sat down again, grabbed my chair by the feet and pulled it towards him. "Have no fear! There's no reason, we'll just talk," he reassured me. He slowly started stroking my face. I turned away, I didn't want this. He took the full glass with both hands and put it to my lips. He didn't care about my desperate looks. "You'll drink this to the last drop and feel a lot better afterwards," he promised me. Then he pulled me by my hair... Although I resisted, he stubbornly made me drink.

He kept drinking, I heard her crying from Leyla's room, she was scared and didn't dare to come to me. The man just picked me up and took me to the kitchen counter. He stood behind me and began to explore my body with his hands. I could feel his breath on my neck. The more I fought and protested, the more violent it became. "You're making me do things I don't want to do, I don't want to hurt you," he whispered hoarsely. However, I didn't want to experience this moment, I didn't want to... Damn it, I didn't want to...!

While telling this, Yasemin almost drowned in her tears. Her sobs grew louder and louder... She couldn't control her tears.

To keep me still, he grabbed a towel that was lying on the counter. He was still behind me, holding me so tight against the counter that I couldn't move. He tied my hands behind my back, then my feet. I struggled as he tied me down, pushing against his hands while screaming. To silence me, he covered my mouth. "Do not Cry! I'm hurting you because you're giving me no choice, but if you relax you might not even be in this situation," he told me. I was still standing in the kitchen with my feet and hands tied. He turned my tear-streaked face towards him. I was a victim, I was a kid. My father couldn't intervene... Because he didn't even know where I was. He picked up the glass from the table. "I'll make you drink this. For your peace of mind, because I'm thinking of you, I don't want to harm you, I don't want to hurt you," he lied.

He put the glass on the counter then his hands wandered over my face and body. I could not move. This tall man was pinning my tiny body against the counter. I felt his breath on the back of my neck again, constantly trying to push it away with my head. I fought doggedly to prevent it. But it was useless. Everything was meaningless. I cried all the time.

At that moment I was in such a bad situation that I couldn't think about Leyla. At a very young age I struggled with my own destiny. He pulled me back by my hair and pressed his whole body against me. He held the glass to my mouth. His disgusting gaze was directed at me. "You will drink this,

I will pour it for you now. If you drink it, you won't feel any pain," he said to me. "Don't do it, don't do it, don't do it, Uncle Ferhat," I begged. "If you want me to stop, drink," he said firmly. He angrily held the glass to my mouth. He pulled me by the hair and forced me to swallow. Then I drank again and again and more and more. "Did you see I didn't do anything you didn't want to do while you were drinking?" he said. Then he poured another glass and brought it to me. He didn't care that I begged and cried.

"Do you know how nicely we would get along if you weren't so stubborn," he accused me and let me finish the second glass. I got dizzy, I felt very bad. I didn't want to drink any more. The alcohol had a very bad effect on my childhood body. After the second glass was empty, he took me on his lap. "Are you all right? You're mad. I told you to relax,' he said. A filled third glass stood on the table. I cried helplessly. After a big sip, he put his hands back on my shoulders and started stroking me. I couldn't intervene because of the effect of the drink, but I was aware of everything. Suddenly Leyla opened her room door crying, she didn't come closer because she was too cowardly. "Don't touch the girl, you're drunk. Don't do anything you'll regret later, please. It's not her fault, she's just a kid," she whimpered in terror.

This wild animal, which pulled its hands from my shoulders, suddenly stepped towards Leyla. I wasn't able to intervene.

My hands and feet were still tied. My eyes wandered to the room with the open door. I heard a few beats. Another sound reached my ears, like something had hit the wall. Leyla, she stopped crying, there was silence. I could hear the bed creaking. what happened there? I remembered screaming internally as the wild animal left the room as if nothing had happened. He locked Layla's door and pocketed the key.

This man was a psychopath. He was ill like the other members of his family. What had he done to Leyla? She had fallen silent, I cried for her and for myself. Again he approached me, swayed behind me and put his dirty hands back on my shoulders. I didn't know what he was doing behind me, that was the scariest thing. I turned my head with an effort and saw him take off his sweatpants. All that was left was to pray. Suddenly he stood in front of me in his underwear. I was desperate, didn't know what to do and was filled with shame and fear mixed together.

He brought a handkerchief and wiped both my tears and my nose. "Look, if you drink that third glass, you'll stop crying, believe me. You will feel very comfortable. I won't hurt you but you protest, you're very stubborn, that makes me angry. Then you will say that I hurt you. Remember that and drink the last glass without me having to use force," he demanded. I didn't obey and he yelled outraged, "Do you know what you're making me do? But there is a good solution for you!

What do I have to do?" he yelled. This family was sick and should be treated. I had no more strength. I remembered that I was slowly losing consciousness. I was only 13 years old!

While Yasemin said the last sentence, she got up. I witnessed a tense and angry moment. Her voice grew louder. It was the voice of a victim of injustice, raised as if to demand accountability. I took the recorder and stopped recording because that was the right thing to do at that moment. In her anger, Yasemin looked at me in surprise. "You talk about us being victims of social oppression and you silence me," she said indignantly. Yes, but I found my behavior correct in my own way, unaffected by social pressure. "Yasemin, when you were young you had an unbelievable nightmare. We should now act even more consciously, because how long have you not spoken about these topics? You are traumatized by your past. Are you sure you want me to put the recordings on paper? Do you want me to write them down? Are you ready to announce all your experiences? Are you sure you really want me to publish Yasemin? If you're sure, let's go ahead, but if you later regret it, let's abandon this book project. Let's talk normally, I'm with you and I'm always by your side. Tell me anything you want without a tape recorder."

Yasemin immediately replied: "I am sure and very determined. There is a bond between us, we have built trust in each other. I don't even sit on the balcony because my neighbor might hear it. Just like your example, I'm choking on the fact that we're in a state of social pressure.

Let the wrongdoers suffer their punishment. I am sure and determined. Announce my voice to be heard..."

There was a slight pause, then Yasemin continued: "Publish one voice from hundreds of victims. I want to tell everyone what happened to me. But we had it certified in the presence of a notary that for our safety you are not allowed to mention my real name or that of my brother and sister." Yasemin was right and I took the necessary steps at the notary. The safety of these three people had to be preserved. It was sanctioned that personal data could not be presented in the form of testimony, evidence and verification. Since I wanted to be absolutely sure, I asked Yasemin again: "Do you really want that? It wouldn't suit either of us to break off halfway." But Yasemin was determined. Wanting to make her voice heard, she replied, "Don't let Yasemin's daisies and roses dry out." While I was talking to Yasemin about this, there was a knock on the door. "We're going out, do you have a wish?" the children asked. "No, everything is in the house, don't be late, take the phone with you and answer it when you get a call," Yasemin admonished the children before they left.

Our tea glasses were empty, there were many things to tell. I refreshed our teas, but Yasemin brought cold drinks to the table. Again we both took our places and Yasemin asked: "Are you ready?" "I'm ready!" I answered and started the recorder lying on the table. She continued where she left off without skipping anything:

He started throwing the pillows on the sofa against the walls. In his anger and nervousness he threw everything he could get his hands on. I was very scared. More than you could think. He was dizzy, tense and angry. He did his best to make me drink the third glass. He slowly took a sip from the glass, then suddenly, he wrapped my hair around his finger and quickly pulled my head back, trying to force me to drink. Those two glasses had shaken me and made me almost immobile. It was the first time I drank alcohol. While I tried to sip from the glass in his hand, he ignored my cries for help and objections. I could feel his evil breath, taste the smell of his skin in my mouth.

I was disgusted! Every once in a while he would put the glass on the table, step behind me and touch my shoulder, then run his arms along my breasts. My objections and screams were futile. He quickly turned the chair so that I was facing him. He was right in front of me. I tried to take my eyes off him, I struggled, I was afraid... Despite all my resistance, he didn't stop. His breath and touch were on my neck, he started kissing me. I begged and begged him to stop. "Uncle Ferhat! Uncle Ferhat! Please let me go, please let me go," I whimpered. He didn't want to hear me because he enjoyed my pleading.

He moved his hands over my tiny body, his lips and beard were either on my face or on my neck. He pulled hard on my hair again and gave me the last sips of the glass one at a time. I was still tearful and desperate. I wasn't myself anymore. I experienced the effects of his forced drink. He picked me up in his arms and carried me into the room where I had spent the previous night. I remembered very well that my plea was continued. He had turned me slightly to the side and undid the knotted ties on my arms and feet. I was wearing the baggy sweater from last night. My destiny was a monster. He was mad at me, my struggles were in vain. I tried to push him away to resist.

He held my wrists with one hand and tried to pull off my shalwar with the other. As I began to scream, he covered my mouth and continued to undress me to fulfill his dirty ambitions. I was just a girl resisting and struggling while he was trying to get my body. "Call me uncle, call me uncle," he kept repeating. What kind of perversion did he have no conscience? How could a person do these things to a small child? He had ignored my crying, begging and screaming. He held me tight. There was nothing I could do. After hours of torture, he raped me. I was raped by Uncle Ferhat after morning prayer...

"Have you filed a criminal complaint?" I asked.

"I was in a village, what could I do? What crime should I have complained about?' she said. "Have you gone to the prosecutor's office?" I asked further. "Yes, I am, but the prosecutor was a relative of my father-in-law. They turned it into a libel suit. I was shocked, what justice was that? What was that law they ended up punishing a little girl who was the victim?" Not wanting to interrupt Yasemin, I said, "Please go on."

"It doesn't matter, I'll talk about those subjects later. I was slowly recovering from the rape. I cried loudly and drunk on the sofa: "Why, why did you do that, you criminal? You raped me why did you do that to me? Why did you kill me? Why did you take my future away from me? You ruined me!" I started screaming. The echo of my screams came back to me from the empty rooms. My hands and feet were no longer tied, I felt freer. Luckily he wasn't with me anymore, which gave me more strength to scream.

I went to the bathroom, Leyla was still locked in her room. There was a knock on the door. Not one, but a few people were standing in front of the front door early in the morning.

I was still wearing the shalwar, which I hadn't taken off since last night. I kept sobbing when I reached the door. The rapist rushed at me from the bedroom and started hitting me with all his might. The speed of the tapping gradually increased. The clan stood greedily in front of the apartment door. "Open the door! Open the door, my son," the fox called to us. The screams got louder, but he left me and poured himself another glass of raki, downed it in one gulp and lay down on the bed where he had raped me. He fell asleep immediately.

I took the opportunity of the moment and locked him in. Those in front of the door were bad people. That's why I didn't care about them, I wanted to go to Leyla first. The young woman was still in bed. I woke her up with a shake. The first thing she said was, "I hope he didn't hurt you, my poor child..." At that moment we both hugged each other and wept. "Come on, we have to pack," she prompted, holding my head up. She had made me a strong cup of coffee in a hurry. With her other hand she covered the wounds on her body. The front of the door was still under siege. The screams echoed inside us. I was tearful, scared and shy... Wherever Leyla went, I followed her and held her with one hand.

However, she found herself in a difficult situation and was a victim herself. But for me she was the strong one at the moment and that felt good. Although I saw that she was also a victim, her determination made me brave. But I couldn't recover. The mother-in-law, the vixen keeps knocking on the door. "What's going on, what's going on? What have you two done to my son?" she shrieked. We hadn't done anything, but her son did us both great harm. Would a person with such an attitude help us if we opened the door? Or would we be in even bigger trouble? We were both excited and scared, but still my eyes closed with exhaustion and weakness. I was supposed to be sleeping, but we had to get out of here. "He's not like that, how could he do something like that?" I kept saying.

Eventually my eyes closed and I fell asleep. Leyla woke me up: "Get up, wash yourself, I'll open the door." I quickly washed my hands and face, I felt tired and was sleepy. I did my best to wake up. I should have been strong, got out of this house, and filed a criminal complaint with the police. My fight wouldn't be easy, but I had to do it. Leyla quietly unlocked the room where her husband slept. Luckily he was still asleep. She closed the door again and softly motioned for me to come over to her.

The outer door was open and she pulled me protectively behind her with one hand. Her mother-in-law rushed into the apartment as soon as the door opened. "Where is my son? Where's my son?" she wailed, quickly pushing us aside. I was still hiding behind Leyla. She opened the doors to all the rooms and looked for her son. Leyla was very calm at that moment, she said: "Mother, you are too loud. You will wake up your son. He's over there." She had entered his room and hurried to the sofa, checking his heart rate. The world was upside down, she thought we had tortured her son when he had been torturing us. "Who did the voices come from? she asked us angrily. "I went to the bathroom," I fibbed. Leyla immediately spoke up: "The girl was afraid when she suddenly met Ferhat in the dark. He got up at night and kept drinking.

He got angry and yelled at Yasemin." "Leave my son alone, don't bother him, don't bother him," the vixen snapped at us. Leyla, who was closing the outer door, turned to me and said: "Yasemin, didn't I tell you to be quiet. I'll take care of it." Why hadn't Leyla told what happened that night? That confused me. She had locked the room where her husband slept. "We have to stay calm," she murmured frantically and excitedly. "We have to find a solution." But Leyla had forgotten something, that I was no longer the Yasemin of yesterday, no longer the flawless Yasemin. She knew that, but she still wanted to confront me about him to find a solution. So Leyla was also mentally unstable.

I noticed that at that moment. I had to go to the police immediately and file a criminal complaint while the crime was still fresh. It was shortly before noon, Ferhat was still asleep.

Time seemed to stand still. Waiting for his awakening was like death for me. At times I couldn't control my tears. People kept coming and going. "Come, sit next to me, let's talk," Leyla asked me. I willingly went to her and sat down. I was afraid of what would happen to me from now on. What did you tell my father? How could I prove my innocence? Very difficult moments awaited me. As I sat next to Leyla, she told me everything one after the other:

"The intention was banal, they unleashed everything bad that exists on us. Believe me, my husband is not like that. He scolds, we're having a fight, yes, but to this day he hasn't even raised his hand. He was drunk at our wedding and yesterday. He doesn't really drink, so he must have been forced into it." "Nothing you're saying can excuse what he did to me," I interrupted through sobs. "You can obey, but I don't have to. I was brought here against my will. I was kidnapped!

He took my childhood from me, how am I ever going to be able to look at my father's face again? Do you know what he did to me?" Someone tried to open the door. Leyla immediately jumped up from her seat and headed for the door. "I have some things I need to talk to you about. I'll come to your room later," she said hastily. She made coffee and a glass of water, then entered Ferhat's room without objection. I was surprised. The world couldn't be more different yesterday and today...

I didn't know what they were talking about. I was scared, very scared. My heart was pounding with excitement.

The minutes that passed seemed like hours. While waiting, I finally heard Uncle Ferhat's voice after 15-20 minutes. "Can not be! Can not be! It can't be!' screams came from the room. Uncle Ferhat cried! What had Leyla told him? My fear subsided when I heard him crying like that, and my shyness gave way to courage. Someone approached me. I could hear footsteps. I was nervous but braver this time. He stood in front of me, this villain. He covered his face and mouth with his hands, his eyes bloodshot from crying. He repeats the same thing over and over again without taking his hands off his face. "Can not be! Can not be! What have I done, what have I done, oh God?" He was shocked. Leyla followed him and stepped behind me.

I didn't expect to experience such a scenario, I was shocked. Leyla held my shoulders and strengthened my back. "I am behind you, you are not alone. I'm here, don't be afraid," she repeated. She was knocked down, pushed and kicked, but she was very strong. She had a clear conscience and compassion that others lacked. She did not tolerate injustice. I had experienced days that cannot be erased from my memory and left deep wounds in my soul. I hugged Leyla crying. "Why did you do this to me, why did you ruin my future?

You destroyed all my dreams and my future. Shame on you all. I refer you to God," I said. Uncle Ferhat took his eyes off us, fell on his knees, sobbed, and hid his face in his hands again.

At that moment I couldn't control my emotions, I let go of Leyla and started punching Uncle Ferhat in the back. The more I hit, the more his hiccups grew. "Why, why, why?" I yelled and kept hitting him, he didn't fight back. Leyla cried with me. "What's happening to us? Wasn't it all because of your mother!" Leyla complained. I wanted to go to the police, I wanted to complain about him and everyone else. Leyla challenged me: "Come wash your face, our day is longer than expected. We will take the girl home to her father and let her go to the police. If you don't go, I'll call the police here," Leyla promised.

Leyla, who was humiliated by everyone yesterday, was stronger than all of them at that moment! "We're going, okay! Whatever my punishment, I will accept it," Ferhat said, standing up. He was still sobbing when he went to the sink to wash his hands and face. "You saw his condition, he was under the influence of alcohol," Leyla reminded me. That couldn't be an excuse for anything. They had ruined my life and they were guilty of bringing me here. How would I be able to see my father's face? How should I return? I was dishonored and wept in despair.

It was almost five o'clock and it was getting late in the evening. Impatience swirled around me, hunger gnawed at me, but I was unable to think about food. I was sleep deprived and had bruises all over my body that were painful.

The wound opened in the heart never closes.
It only connects the top to the shell.
The mark underneath remains intact...

CHAPTER
11

Despite all the questions, we were able to leave the house without making noise. That was my salvation. I didn't even look behind and got in the car with Leyla. Ferhat finally got in the car. 'The curtain moved. "We're being watched," Leyla whispered, startled. The front door opened and Uncle Ferhat's brother appeared. "Brother, are you all right?" he asked. "We've got work to do, and we'll return when we're done," he said calmly.

Suddenly the brother went to the car and told "You sit in the back," to his sister-in-law. She got out and sat next to me without objection. He got in the front. "Now we're done, pray!" she whispered to me, taking my hand and praying. After a long drive, Ferhat parked the car. It was a crowded street, I had never been there. "Well, we're there, where do you have to go?" Ferhat asked.

"I've brought a lot of time with me and I'll go with you. Maybe you'll run into her father or relatives, you won't be alone,' he offered. Uncle Ferhat didn't object to that, he seemed a bit desperate to me. The two went ahead and we behind them. "I think we drove here to distract him, there's no police station here," she whispered to me softly.

Yasemin switched off the tape recorder again. "Come on, let's take a break. We started well, she yawned. We both sat back and drank our tea. It was over for today, Yasemin would start working again tomorrow."

The next day at noon I went to the cinema with the children. It was almost evening when we got home. We had a meal and we had amazing night laughs, jokes and chat. Later the children went to bed, my brother, Yasemin and I talked for a while on the balcony. At around 10.45am my brother wished us good night then left us alone. "Fortunately, our Lord brought me together with you. I'm glad I met you guys. You're doing us a lot of good", Yasemin spoke softly. It was also good for us, since we weren't tired yet, we continued to talk. As the weather cooled, we grabbed a blanket from inside and snuggled up by candlelight. Our teas and the tape recorder were on the table.

"Do you think others will read my story and gain strength from it? Will my story give them a way of hope? Will they find the strength to escape from the people who harm them and darken their days?" she sighed, bowing her head slightly and eyes hopeful. Publish! Announce my story at all costs.

You gave me strength, you became my hope. You got me out of my impasse even though you didn't realize it. Thank God I haven't gone insane. While I was struggling desperately for our lives with my siblings, You met us with trust, compassion and warmth. Although you suffered a heavy blow of life and took in your brother. How did you achieve that? What power is this? What a success!"

I replied to Yasemin as follows: "If God allows, I can publish it. Everything is in God's protection, everything will happen by God's will and only by his will. It's not just about will, we will try. From time to time you will succumb to your pain, feel tired, cry, maybe even laugh while you tell me everything. It's not easy to tell about your pain, nightmare days, trauma and resistance. If you really want to do this, we will ask our Lord for strength."

Yasemin stood slowly from her seat and hugged me. We had embarked on an exciting and difficult path, but she kept telling.

Leyla said to me quietly and confused, "I assume he wants to stop him. This road does not lead to the police station."

So we walked down the main street lined with shops, markets and boutiques. There weren't such long and wide streets in our village, it was far too crowded. I didn't want to waste my time wandering around with them. I had been beaten, bullied and raped, I was in pain and wounds, I was exhausted. Leyla worriedly held my hand. We followed the two, who were talking in whispers. Uncle Ferhat was distracted, he wasn't himself. He walked into a restaurant unconscious, half dead, half alive, but I didn't want to see his face. I was amazed at how patiently I could endure him today even though I hated him so much. I said today, I hope my Lord will not let me experience those days again. (Amen)

Yasemin, you said 'today'. How would you act today?" I asked her. "That's a good question," she replied. "I would probably scream until my lungs burned, until my breath stopped. I would have been screaming for help for so long today. I wouldn't walk down the whole street, that's for sure."

But you know it's not easy. I was hoping we would do what we discussed at home, that he go to the police and plead guilty. For taking me to my father's as promised." "Don't blame yourself, it's not your fault, Yasemin," I emphasized. "In this case you did what had to be done. The steps you took were for your own safety. It's not your fault, you see. Don't take the blame." "That's easy to say. I wish I'd screamed for help on that street. I've been kidnapped, help! If only I had screamed that they were so bad, if only they had been arrested at that moment," she lamented. She shook off the thoughts briefly, then picked up the thread again.

They entered a restaurant and we followed them. Uncle Ferhat whispered something in Leyla's ear. She just answered him with a nod before we sat down. I shook Leyla's arm slightly and asked: "What happened, what did he say?" "Later!" she whispered to me. After we all got to the table, Uncle Ferhat said, "Order the food, I'll park the car in front of the entrance."

The bad brother sat in front of me, Leyla and I next to each other. We couldn't talk because of him. My back was to the entrance, although I was hungry I couldn't eat because of the nightmares.

Almost half an hour later Uncle Ferhat did not return. He had ordered beans with rice. Suddenly he said he forgot something in the car. He went to the wagon and his brother followed him. Leyla and I sat alone at the table. "When will we go? What happens there? Let's go now! Why is this murderous man coming with us?" I said angrily. "Drop your desperation," Leyla reassured me, but I was panicking. Suddenly Uncle Ferhat called Leyla from the entrance and asked for something from the car. Confused, Leyla replied, "I didn't touch it, it's still in the car." "Come and see where it is," he persisted. Leyla followed him without objection. When I turned back, no one was there except for the patrons and the restaurant staff. I was afraid! I looked back from time to time, Leyla was still absent.

You don't need to listen to a person's screams.
You can read his life with your eyes,
hear it with your mind, and feel it with your heart.
Just want to see and hear.

Yasemin's Desperation

CHAPTER
12

After a while , nobody came. I didn't have a watch and sat ignorant. I asked the waiter who came to clear the table. "Where are they?" He checked and replied, "The three of them were just in the car out front, but now there's neither of them nor the car." It felt like boiling water was being poured over my head. I was worried because I didn't have 5 lira in my pocket. I immediately went to the waiter and asked him, "Please help me." I roughly explained the situation to him. "Please call the police immediately," I begged him, crying. "Wait, come in here, have a water. Calm down, we'll call the police, don't worry!" he said. I was tired of having to wait everywhere. Everyone made decisions for me. "No, why should I wait? Please call the police, a crime has been committed here," I said angrily. A couple from the next table, whose attention I caught, got up and came to my side. "What happened, why don't they call the police?" he asked the waiter with concern. Thanks to this customer, he immediately called the police. He gave the name and address of the restaurant. "We have a concern. The situation is explosive, we're worried, something happened," he said, I remembered it well. I sat at the couple's table and waited for the police. They kept asking me questions, but I was in tears. I had to leave the restaurant as soon as possible in case Ferhat would come back at any moment.

Finally the police arrived about 15 to 20 minutes later. I was relieved when I saw her. I ran to them and, excited and in tears, started telling what had happened to me. They asked for my identity. "They have my ID at their house," I reported. "How did you get here?" More questions followed. "I'll tell them everything. Please take me safely to the police station. I will tell you everything there. Let's get out of here?" I begged him.

After they took my testimony, which village I was from and my name, they sent the information to the police. They obtained confirmation of my identity and took me to the police station. I sat in the back of the police car, sobbing over and over again and expressing my gratitude. I thought I was saved.

They asked questions about my father. "Call my father, he'll come right away," I asked him. I gave our house number. Then they told me to wait in the hallway. I sat shyly in the aisle, waiting and crying. I had always thought about what to say when my father came. How am I supposed to look at his face? Surely he worried? It was great that they called. I thought they allayed my dad's concern, but it turns out my world was turned upside down.

A police officer called me, "Come with me to make your statement." Another officer, probably a detective, was sitting with a typewriter. "We called your father, he'll come here.

You're under 18, you won't be able to testify until your guardian comes," he lectured me.

I had no other choice, I had to wait for my father. "But I can't tell those nightmarish moments in front of my father," I protested. "You are underage. After your father's signature, he can wait outside the door. Go back into the corridor, wait there," he told me.

"If her father comes, let me know immediately," he said to a colleague. My body shook with insomnia, hunger and excitement.

My father still wasn't there...

While I was waiting, an officer gave me water. I emptied it in one gulp. A few hours passed, my father didn't come. I walked up to the first police officer I saw and asked, "Can you call home again?"

"Your father is on his way," he replied. "Who were you on the phone with?" I asked. "With a man," he said.

As I was walking to my seat in the hallway, my father came. With great joy I immediately called out: "Father!"

My salvation had come, my hero. My father, on the other hand, was in an explosive state like ignited gunpowder.

I was afraid! Was he mad at me or at them? It was awful to think about it and not know the answer. Very nervous, he approached me with huge strides without saying anything, without changing the expression on his face, without taking his eyes off me. At that moment, for the first time, I felt a fear of my father that I had never had before.

When he came to me he raised his hand. With all his might he gave me the biggest hit of my life. "You little idiot! You have violated the honor, reputation and chastity of our family! How you did it! Haven't you even thought about your family's honor!" he yelled at me. Even though I was on the ground, he kept hitting me.

I was shocked. It wasn't until the police pulled my father away from me that he stopped.

"Lie! Lie! I haven't done anything. My stepmother sold me, it's not my fault. Believe me daddy, believe me daddy, I haven't done anything. He raped me, my stepmother gave me to them with her own hands. I didn't know about them, they kidnapped me. Believe me, Papa!" I roared hoarsely.

My father cursed me: "Damn it, you slander your mother without shame. There is no place where she has not looked for you. She was unhappy because she hadn't found you. She hadn't slept all night because she was worried and you are slandering her. Shame on my daughter! Couldn't you wait to get out of the splendid father's house?"

Not one statement my father made was true. They slandered me. My father accused me and every harsh word he said pierced my heart like a dagger. At that young age, my heart bled. I was devastated...

I had no strength to stand, no strength to do anything, and sat on the floor, leaning against the wall. I sobbed and covered my face with my hands. "You lie, lie, don't slander me," I said as loudly as I could. My father, on the other hand, tried to calm down but continued to swear.

That was enough. I only had one father and they took him away from me. My world has been destroyed.

My father promised the officers: "My nerves have calmed down. I calmed down. I promise I won't do anything, I've calmed down." Then he approached me. I broke down for fear of my father.

He quietly insulted me, he sat next to me on the chair. My chest burned, my heart bled. Every time I tried to say something, he yelled, "Beauty! you are disrespectful. You've damaged our reputation, honor. With that courage do you speak? I have no daughter."

The officer wouldn't let my father go. "Your daughter will have to testify. We need her signature since she's not adult," he said. "You won't testify, I'll tell them what they want to hear. I will not allow you to humiliate our family and our honor again," he snapped.

He was always interrupting me, always interrupting me, not allowing me to speak. "Father, they betrayed you, don't believe what you were told," I sobbed. But he kept saying, "Shut up! Dress up! You made me bow my head." He kept talking, ignoring me.

He explained to the detective as follows: "We don't need to scale up the case. It's not what we thought. The suspect and my daughter fell in love and fled without our will. I told his family that I would not give my daughter to him until she was of legal age. They acted secretly and ran away.

My daughter lied to them saying our house didn't have a phone so she couldn't be taken back. My daughter's mother passed away. As you can see, we are here now, sir. Nothing happened to my daughter. She was afraid of me and only says so because otherwise she would be taken home."

I cried the whole time and tried to signal to the officer that I didn't corroborate his statement. None of this was true. According to my father, the inspector asked me, "Is that correct?"

I couldn't answer, so he repeated, "I'm asking you, is what your father said true?" He had asked exactly three times. Then my father raised his voice: "Answer, the chief of police is waiting for your answer. By not answering you make me a liar. Confirm what I said! Come on, confirm it!" At that moment I was desperate and I confirmed: 'Yes, it's the truth.'

After confirming his incorrect statement, I couldn't control my sobs.

"Then sign your statement and stop bothering the police with such things. Solve your family problems in the family!' he said harshly. However, it was understood from every angle that I had made a false statement.

Wars don't just happen on the front lines,
they happen in the heart.

Yasemin's Desperation

CHAPTER
13

This was the first time I had seen and experienced my father so upset. It was the first time I was so afraid of him. My father wasn't like that, how could they have deceived him like that? His change hurt more than my wounds and injuries.

We had left the commissioner's office. My father pulled my arm with great anger to get us out of the station as quickly as possible. And I - I confess with cynicism - really wanted to get away from my father's side at that moment. We quickly walked towards the car. Two older men I knew from the village were standing next to the car. My father did not come alone. That wasn't good at all. "Get in!" he ordered me. Nervously, even aggressively, my father nudged me. I sat in the back seat without answering.

My father was still angry and didn't think about what the three older men would think of me. I didn't understand why he believed the lies. He was driving way too fast, which frightened me in every way.

I thought we were going home. We had been on the road for almost an hour and a half. Our village was far away from the city. My father continued to be angry. There was no description for my mood.

The man sitting in front said, "Your mother wasn't like that.

I wonder why she's turned out like this?" With that, I felt pinned to the wall.

"Don't talk about my mother, use common sense!" I sobbed. My father's anger did not stop. He pulled over, forced me out, leaned me against the car and hit me. "See what you hear from the others. What am I hearing about you? Look at the troubles you caused me! Little slut! Couldn't you wait to come of age? I dishonor you, little prostitute!" he threw at me.

"It's not my fault, they betrayed you. My stepmother brought me to them with her own hands. Why do not you believe me? Why don't you listen to me?" I howled. My father should have believed me because I wasn't lying. It was dark, the drivers who passed us noticed that I was being hit and honked their horns or flashed their headlights. He forced me back into the car and we drove on. "You embarrassed me in front of passers-by too," he accused me.

I cried... couldn't believe what was going on. My father's behavior shocked me. I couldn't think of anything else.

The slightly younger man sitting next to me in the back stroked my hand unobtrusively. I immediately pulled them away, I was shocked. But he didn't let go, came closer again and this time started to touch my arm.

"What are you doing?" I asked tearfully, looking at him in surprise. With his eyebrow he motioned me to be silent. Then he stroked my leg.

"Enough, that's enough! Take your hand off me," I yelled at him. He immediately protected himself with the following words: "I wanted to comfort her so that she would stop crying. I gave her a handkerchief. Have I done something bad?"

However, there was no handkerchief, it was also a lie. I wanted to get out of the car and away from everyone as quickly as possible. He took advantage of my father's position. I couldn't see the street properly because of the tears, but I was sure it wasn't our village. "Dad, aren't we going home?" I asked, horrified.

"Don't call me dad. I no longer have a daughter like you. You have trampled on our honor. If I bring you back home I'll be damned!" he spat out hard.

I didn't know the feeling of being paralyzed in my body, but after my father's hurtful words I felt numbness.

They are the experiences that determine the path of man...

Yasemin's Desperation

CHAPTER
14

My own father was one of the people who let me go through this trauma.

He was ruthless. I begged in the car, "Father, please don't hand me over to these people. Dad, please don't give me to them. You have caused me a lot of bad damage. It was your wife who cheated on you and handed me over. It's your wife telling you the lies. The man I was promised to is married! You ruined my future!" I screamed so loud it would tear down a wall. But my father's heart seemed petrified.

We were there. The men were standing in front This was the first time I had seen and experienced my father so upset. It was the first time I was so afraid of him. My father wasn't like that, how could they have deceived him like that? His change hurt more than my wounds and injuries.

We had left the commissioner's office. My father pulled my arm with great anger to get us out of the station as quickly as possible. And I - I confess with cynicism - really wanted to get away from my father's side at that moment. We quickly walked towards the car. Two older men I knew from the village were standing next to the car. My father did not come alone. That wasn't good at all. "Get in!" he ordered me. Nervously, even aggressively, my father nudged me. I sat in the back seat without answering.

My father was still angry and didn't think about what the three older men would think of me. I didn't understand why he believed the lies. He was driving way too fast, which frightened me in every way.

I thought we were going home. We had been on the road for almost an hour and a half. Our village was far away from the city. My father continued to be angry. There was no description for my mood.

The man sitting in front said, "Your mother wasn't like that. I wonder why she's turned out like this?" With that, I felt pinned to the wall.

"Don't talk about my mother, use common sense!" I sobbed. My father's anger did not stop. He pulled over, forced me out, leaned me against the car and hit me. "See what you hear from the others. What am I hearing about you? Look at the troubles you caused me! Little slut! Couldn't you wait to come of age? I dishonor you, little prostitute!" he threw at me.

"It's not my fault, they betrayed you. My stepmother brought me to them with her own hands. Why do not you believe me? Why don't you listen to me?" I howled. My father should have believed me because I wasn't lying. It was dark, the drivers who passed us noticed that I was being hit and honked their horns or flashed their headlights. He forced me back into the car and we drove on. "You embarrassed me in front of passers-by too," he accused me.

I cried... couldn't believe what was going on. My father's behavior shocked me. I couldn't think of anything else.

The slightly younger man sitting next to me in the back stroked my hand unobtrusively. I immediately pulled them away, I was shocked. But he didn't let go, came closer again and this time started to touch my arm.

"What are you doing?" I asked tearfully, looking at him in surprise. With his eyebrow he motioned me to be silent. Then he stroked my leg.

"Enough, that's enough! Take your hand off me," I yelled at him. He immediately protected himself with the following words: "I wanted to comfort her so that she would stop crying. I gave her a handkerchief. Have I done something bad?"

However, there was no handkerchief, it was also a lie. I wanted to get out of the car and away from everyone as quickly as possible. He took advantage of my father's position. I couldn't see the street properly because of the tears, but I was sure it wasn't our village. "Dad, aren't we going home?" I asked, horrified.

"Don't call me dad. I no longer have a daughter like you. You have trampled on our honor. If I bring you back home I'll be damned!" he spat out hard.

I didn't know the feeling of being paralyzed in my body, but after my father's hurtful words I felt numbness.

of Ferhat's front door, and the women were looking out the window. It was obvious that they had been waiting for us.

"I have come to restore your honor," my father said. They insulted me. I was in a miserable state, but no one cared. No one! My father just drove off and I was under their patronage. My only protector was God. Besides him I had no one to seek refuge with.

No matter how old a person was, this type of cruelty was not and could not be condoned. I didn't want to believe what was happening to me and my father.

Now I was back in that horrible house where I had had those nightmarish moments. I was exhausted, hurt, had even lost my father. My strength, energy and reserves were exhausted.

Leyla didn't come downstairs, I hadn't seen her yet.

"Oh, what happened to us, what happened to us...?" the women of the house kept wailing, beating their knees. I didn't understand what happened or had happened to them. Because it happened to me.

The crowd dispersed. The fox nudged me and uttered the proverb: "The inhabitants of their villages are the owners of their houses." So to say, I should go to my future apartment.

They forcibly brought me into the apartment. As if nothing had ever happened, I had to go back to my nightmare. Brought here by my own father this time. Leyla opened the door, but I refused to move into the room where I was being deflowered against my will. I protested, then finally she took me to another room. It was like a storage room, there was no place to sleep. "I'll fix it for you tomorrow. Can you spend a night in the other room?" she asked me. Did I even have a choice?

It was three o'clock in the morning, I was exhausted, battered and badly wounded. I locked the door. As soon as I entered, the torture I had endured flashed before my eyes. I couldn't sleep in the bed and lay down on the hard floor.

At first I had trouble sleeping. "Mom, Mom," I cried. I searched for my mother's arms, her wings, her protection above all her love and affection. You could tell how desperate I was that I was begging for help from my late mother.

In the morning, my pain caused by the beating was made worse by sleeping on the floor without a mattress. From next door I heard the vacuum cleaner. It could only be Leyla, but I was afraid to leave the room. So I waited until she stopped vacuuming and then called her: "Leyla."

"Come out, don't be afraid. There's no one home but us," she told me.

"Why did you leave me there, why didn't you come to the police station with me?" I accused her immediately. "You deceived my father, he rejected me. He brought me here with his own hands. There were false statements at the police station. Why did you allow this? You know I'm not guilty, you see for yourself. Please help me prove this. Help me tell my father the truth, bear witness that I am not a lie and that I am innocent."

Leyla was the only one who could help me.

"Come sit down. Let's talk over breakfast," she offered, hugging me. She brought our breakfast and tea to the table.

Leyla didn't see me as her husband's second wife, but as a victim. Like a worried older sister, she began to say, "Your stepmother ruined you and that witch mother-in-law buried you alive. Believe me, whatever happened to us was because of those two. They ruined your life, destroyed your future, and also brought fire to my home, believe me... You keep calling him uncle. My God is witness, he will not touch you. He is being punished for what he has done, tormented by remorse. He will go and turn himself in to the police. Believe me it will happen. I will help you heal your deep wounds, I am by your side. Because of what happened yesterday I couldn't show you the attention I should have given you when they brought you in at night. Forgive me if I unknowingly hurt you too. You will be saved, from now on you are in good hands. Due to my mother-in-law's pressure, I can't even go to the neighbor's, but we will find a way, I will help you. She had told his brother yesterday that we were going to the police. He then hastily drove us away from there. Ferhat was still ailing, his brother didn't take him seriously. I got used to it. That's why I've learned to ignore it. You must rest first. You must be strong. Believe me, everyone will pay for what they did and they will pay a lot.

Even if you pour out your heart to your father and beg for his mercy, your reputation is gone. They won't put you in the village. All he cares about is his honor, he doesn't care about his daughter. Your father is crying out that his honor is lost. Instead of being a father and supporting you, he brought you back here with his own hands. Yasemin, nobody can do anything for us. We are used to being knocked down, pushed, kicked and humiliated. Look, I don't have a mother either. My father didn't get married, I swear to God. He stood there calmly. I was the only girl in the house, my brothers sold me. I can't escape so will I endure all this trouble? The question is, where do I stay when I go? My hands are tied, I submit to my fate here. Believe me, I suffer the ordeal of life. You're still young, if you're trying to save your life, you have a better chance. I'm behind you, Yasemin, don't be afraid. Come on, have a slice of bread. Who knows how long you haven't eaten. You have to get up."

When Leyla spoke like that, I stayed where I was. I found it right in one way and wrong in another. As she said, there was really nothing that could be done at the moment.

Conscience accounting is the heaviest of accounts...

CHAPTER
15

Almost a month had passed. That month I saw uncle Ferhat few times it was not more than the numbers of fingers of a hand. It was a coincidence when we met in the corridor, on the stairs, or when entering and exiting the room. Even when I looked at him, he immediately took his eyes off me. Not once - I can't lie - had he looked at me. He left the house when I woke up and came home when I was in bed.

I started doing what Leyla said. I didn't listen to the hurtful words. In fact, I ignored them. I spoke to no one, only forced to answer the questions that asked. There was still no news from my father. I did the housework from morning to night.

Thanks to Leyla, I got another room to sleep in that also had to be locked. Leyla kept saying to me, "Yasemin, always tell me when you bleed. Don't let my mother-in-law hear it. Otherwise she'll ask for a child." She was right, she didn't want to hear that. Over time, the vixen managed to get me to call her "mother". Even though there were thousands of needles sticking out of my tongue every time, I had to say it. They always took me to the doctor. They thought I was in a relationship with Uncle Ferhat. Leyla, Uncle Ferhat and I were forced to play this game. "Are you infertile too?" she kept asking.

15 months had now passed. In the house I was a maid. They said "come", I jumped, they ordered "go", then I went. I was a walking dead with a frozen heart and soulless. For nine months they hadn't let me go out the door or into the garden. Only then did they let me into the garden that ran around the house. They chained my feet to keep me from running away! We also had fields, vineyards and gardens. I knew very well how to cultivate from there. I dedicated myself to gardening. It was my remedy, it was very good.

A woman can be destroyed but never give up!

CHAPTER
16

In the meantime my stepmother had given birth to a child. I didn't know Kiraz, my little sister, I hadn't even seen her before...

One day the bitter news came from my father. He had died. They said because of me because he ashamed of his daughter's sins. The thought hurt. "She's going, she's not going!" They argued loudly in the house about whether I could go to the funeral. I didn't have a say, I wasn't allowed to make any decisions. Therefore, I had silently accepted every decision of theirs. When I heard the news of my father's death, I didn't cry much. My heart was petrified at the time, my sanity questionable. My feelings were like death. I was almost depressed and devastated.

They had decided to take me to the funeral. We went with Uncle Ferhat and his brother. Everyone who attended the funeral accused me, "Your father had a heart attack because of you. You put your father in the grave. Your father died because of you.

I didn't even listen to her words, I was numb. My stepmother glanced at me but immediately turned away. She was the head of the snake. She knew the facts, she wasn't able to look at me. I didn't want to stay a second longer and demanded that we drive back.

At home I told Leyla about my soulless and emotionless state. She hugged me and said kindly: "All this will pass, believe me. You don't deserve to live like this. Those who force you to do this will be punished sooner or later. Believe me sooner or later." She always sought refuge in God. The love of God was so ingrained that her eyes lit up every time she spoke about God and love for Him. Her heart was very pure.

Best repair of broken heart;
it's a touch of the soul.

CHAPTER
17

A few days after the funeral, my stepmother, who had never come before or even called, came to visit us. I immediately yelled for Leyla, who immediately rushed over. My half brother Suat sat quietly next to her. Kiraz, on the other hand, had already learned to walk and was jumping around the house. For the first time in a long time I had a feeling in my heart. My half siblings were very cute. I felt something inside of me come alive when I was around her. My stepmother just came to say that she was going through difficult times. Because of the children, she asked for my help.

Since I did not have to decide, they consulted in the house. I ended up packing my suitcase for a week and sat in the car with my stepmother. Uncle Ferhat drove us to my father's house. I was scared but also excited because I had missed my village so much...

We spoke very little, even when we had to. Uncle Ferhat had no respect for my stepmother, yet he never said anything wrong to her. Both played a big part in everything that had happened to me. They were both guilty, they knew it, but didn't say a word.

Uncle Ferhat, still unable to look me in the face as he spoke, pulled me into a room. "You'll call me right away if anything happens," he said and gave me a phone. He wrote his home address and cell phone number on a piece of paper. He briefly explained how to use the phone and which buttons to press.

"I don't trust your stepmother, look, you'll call right away before you get in trouble. Tomorrow I will also bring Leyla here. Come test my phone," he offered. It was the first cell phone I used. Timidly, I dialled the number and Uncle Ferhat rang. "Okay!" he confirmed, then drove off. After all, this was the first time I was alone with my stepmother. My siblings slept in my former room. There had been a few changes in the house. I cried silently, my father was gone. He died because of me! The pain was unbearable because he didn't know his daughter well, it wasn't my fault. "Only those who have experienced it know the pain of losing."

The tape buzzed and turned itself off. This was Yasemin's first full tape recording. While Yasemin talked about this part of her life that had left deep wounds in her heart, she sighed with sadness and sobbed. I hugged her. Her head rested on my shoulder. It was a great success. This man, whom she addressed as Uncle Ferhat, never touched her again. If it were otherwise, she would certainly say so. I wanted to end the conversation for today and Yasemin agreed: "Okay, you're right!" We hadn't realized that it was already three in the morning. Time passed way too quickly.

Yasemin's great storytelling enabled me to visualize. I could picture everything perfectly. She was tired. After we cleaned up, we both got ready for bed and went to sleep. So that Yasemin didn't oversleep and got to work on time, I set my cell phone alarm. In the morning I got up with Yasemin. Due to insomnia and crying, her eyes were slightly swollen. The children were still asleep. I went into the kitchen, made tea, then I prepared the breakfast table. "I don't have breakfast in the morning, I prepare the table and the school bags for my siblings. I'll get ready while they have breakfast," she told me. We had something in common again. Was it healthy? Of course not ... ! We said goodbye, then Yasemin went to work. After breakfast, the children helped me to clean the breakfast table. Then we went to the cinema, not only the children were happy, it was good for me too, even if the film was for the children I enjoyed it. After the film we met up with Yasemin who was on her lunch break. She arrived at the cafeteria half an hour late with the excuse that she had bought cassettes for the tape recorder. It was not yet certain when we would see each other again. At least she was able to take more pictures and then send them to me in the mail. That was a good idea. The joint talks were of course something else, but for the moment this was a good temporary solution despite we enjoyed being together.

Yasemin was constantly worried that she and her siblings would be found. She showed her fear openly. Her address was confidential, no information was released even when she was searched. She had achieved this through a court decision. "Please don't express your fears in front of your siblings," I whispered to her. "Teach them how to protect themselves when I'm at work or not around you," she asked me firmly. "I'm afraid for my siblings, I want them to know that. I emphasize: We have no one but God. Of course we are under his protection, but my lord has given us a memory to use. I want my siblings to know that they would be in a bad way!" I couldn't disagree, Yasemin was right. But her siblings wouldn't understand until she told them clearly what it was like. Although Yasemin only came to Germany five years ago, she spoke German very well. She was enthusiastic, determined and hardworking. As already mentioned, she loved to read. Her world broadened as she read. She even bought German books to further her education. After our trip I was so tired that I lay down and slept for three hours. It wasn't my habit to sleep in the middle of the day, but it had felt good. I woke up refreshed. Yasemin came to me with a tape we had discussed.

"I hope the sequel will come soon. Let's continue our stories like this for a while," she said. Yasemin had found a way to get rid of her problems. It was evening. Suat, Kiraz and I wanted to cook. Yasemin and my brother told jokes on the balcony.

Her laughter made its way into the kitchen. Even Kiraz was surprised. Because she had never had the chance to see her sister so happy and get to know her sister so well. While Suat was peeling off the onions, I remember it very well , he said: "Please don't go, otherwise we will never see my sister so happy again." Yasemin finally found a way to talk! To communicate! Yes, you read that correctly. "COMMUNICATION!" Yasemin, who never wanted to speak on the balcony so that her neighbors wouldn't hear her, told my brother anecdotes with all joy. When I saw these developments, I was very happy. Yasemin was unaware of the joy that came into the house. Even her siblings were very surprised and affected by this happiness. While we were cooking in the kitchen, we too joked with each other. This moment was very precious for me. Since we would be home Sunday morning, we decided to spend every minute of Saturday together. In the evening we wanted to see a movie. The purchase was made and we made all the preparations. Then we sat on the sofa and watched the film.

Some fell asleep, only Suat and I were still awake. But I only kept myself upright because of the afternoon nap. Even my brother snoozed in his place. When the film was over we woke up the three of them and sent them to bed. The morning passed quickly. After saying goodbye, we stood at the main station with our suitcases. Along the way, my brother and

I talked about how wonderful our days were. At home I was very curious about what could be heard on the recording. I wanted to deal with it immediately. When I finished my work, I made myself a coffee. Because of the nice weather I sat on the balcony. I put Yasemin's cassette into the tape recorder, then played it back. As she said it, I literally repeated it. "Hi! You were so tired I was glad you slept. At least you can rest, it will make you good. I said to the children: "Pssst, Nurgül is sleeping, if you make a noise you will wake them up." They retired to their rooms without upsetting me. Murat is with them too. They're playing the console games he gave them. The doors were closed! I took advantage of the favorable moment and retreated to the balcony. I only have water, my Turkish coffee, an ashtray, my cigarettes and my tape recorder that connect us. With your permission, I want to pick up where I left off."

If you remember, I said: "In my father's house, it was the first time after his death that I felt the presence of my heart and my feelings. That's exactly what happened. After taking a deep breath, I cried. How did I get to my father's house? My father was dead. I was a walking dead and I kept crying about what had happened to us. We hadn't spoken to my stepmother yet. I didn't know if she understood how I felt. Anyway...

I couldn't show much warmth to my siblings either. I had fought against my inner world. At that moment I was very busy with myself. My stepmother did not come to me, but she followed me everywhere with her eyes. As I walked the rooms looking for my father's prayer beads, I hid my tears from her. He loved collecting them. I asked my stepmother where they were as I couldn't find them. "It was full and I threw it away!" she answered heartlessly... Ugh! Would a person throw away the prayer beads her husband had accumulated over the years? I well remembered that while I was watching TV in the evenings, my father would take his prayer beads and clean the stones one by one with a special liquid. He treasured his prayer beads very much. It wasn't my intention to get into an argument with her. That's why I didn't say anything. I mean, I didn't actually intend it. Then I asked for the photos of my father and asked me whether there were still pictures of deceased mother. She said "When Suat saw the pictures, I burned them!"

While Yasemin was describing this, she was very nervous and angry. It wasn't difficult for me to understand this state as I knew every tone of her voice between period and comma.

"How can you burn the pictures of my parents? What kind of person are you? I can't believe what you did. You can't have a clear conscience?" I snapped. I remember being angry with her.

But I can't remember what she answered me. Neighbors came to our house. They pulled me towards them. "What a shame, what face are you making?" they roared. Even though they insulted me so much, my stepmother did not intervene. Everything was going very hard for me, all she said was, "She came to help for Mawlid." People were arguing and saying it was a shame... I couldn't remember her exact wording. I couldn't digest this situation myself, they insulted me in my own home. I started arguing with them. What could I do it was a behavior I couldn't change. It was a situation I didn't like but I didn't have to endure them treating and insulting me like that, so I showed them the door. Even if my stepmother heard what was going on, she didn't care. She didn't even step in to help me. Everything was very strange. In the house where I had once experienced warmth, an icy wind had blown that made me chill. The preparations for the funeral hadn't started yet, I couldn't help. I still struggled in my own way. To distract myself, I began to wander through our garden, which surrounded our house like a frame. It was like everyone was waiting for me to go out. They jumped straight at me and harassed me girls just like the men. I was Ömer's daughter, I was a girl in this village. No one saw any disgrace from me for committing none. No one could say I was dishonest. I had committed no dishonesty. But everyone said so. These people dragged innocent people into the dirt. Suddenly I got scared again and went into the house. As I closed the door behind me, the villagers threw stones at the window and whistled whatever they thought of me. They walked around the house. Even married women yelled, "Look at that little tart, as soon as she came she waved her tail to my husband. She had my husband come to her door."

A loving person also appeared. "Shame on you if you are not ashamed of your humanity, fear God!" he cried indignantly. Actually, it wasn't safe for me in this house. I thought about calling Uncle Ferhat. But, no, I had to endure it until I got out of here. "I must be strong, he cannot be trusted. Do not forget! He harmed you, too." That's not how I called. I went to my stepmother. "Why are these people talking about me like that? Do you have an explanation for me?' I asked her. She replied, "I only wanted your good, so I brought you to them, I don't know how it happened," she feigned. But what she said was a lie, because my father had told me at the police station: "She's crazy about you, there's nowhere she hasn't looked for you." Of course, this statement was false. Once again I realized that she was a liar. In the end I called Uncle Ferhat. It was for my own safety. I briefly told him what had happened. "I'm coming, don't worry, I'll be right there," he comforted me for the first time. I went neither to the window nor into the garden. After an hour he was finally there. "Don't tell my stepmother," I begged him, and he didn't.

We retreated to a room. He still couldn't see my face because of what happened. As little as I in his.

I explained what had happened, saying I didn't feel safe and comfortable. "Don't worry, I'll be close to you. I want you to trust me I'll watch the house from the car. Your father has Mawlid, you will not be alone tomorrow. Leyla will come to you. "Well," I said to myself. "You make all the decisions for me anyway. Even the authority to say yes and amen was not my choice. It was destined for me." Meals were to be prepared tomorrow. But we started the prep overnight by pre-cooking most things. At least I wasn't useless anymore, I had work to do. I wasn't used to being idle because I always started cleaning the house as soon as I woke up and then tended the garden until the evening. He gave me the phone but not the charger. I didn't know such a thing was necessary. From where? So the battery died, the phone went dead while I called Uncle Ferhat. "Did you call?" I managed to get out. Imagine that, I was so ignorant even though I loved to read. I didn't know any better then. I asked my stepmother about the house phone. She replied, "I couldn't pay his debts. I'm getting calls from outside, but I can't call anymore." The fear formed a huge knot in my throat.

It was night and we went to sleep. I was lying on the floor bed in the same room with my brother Suat. The light was off and the room was dark. I couldn't sleep for worry and fear. Suddenly small stones were thrown at the window. I looked up, startled. I had no way of informing Uncle Ferhat. A light kept flashing at the window. It didn't bode well, so I lay very still on the floor. The villagers had tried everything they could to pursue me. They had even bothered me at the window. Why did the villagers do this to me? I was disappointed and scared at the same time. Even though I came to the funeral ceremony and I lost my father, they did this to me! I cried because of my misfortune and why the villagers didn't understand me. Why they treated me like this. As I speak about this now, I'm shaken and I still don't understand. Nurgül, I'm sure you understand how confused and upset I am. Years later I understood the strangeness of never having spoken of myself. After Nurgül wrote this book, I knew that one day there would be those who would hear me and read my story. I was sure of that and cannot thank Nurgül enough for giving me that confidence.

My gratitude increases day by day. Glad I met her. Fortunately, our destiny also had the convergence of our paths ...

The crowd dispersed after a while. When the voices stopped calling, I finally fell asleep. When I woke up in the morning, everyone was already awake. The door was wide open, I got scared. I closed it immediately. When I asked my stepmother if she had heard what was going on outside at night, she replied,

"I hear what I want to hear and ignore the things I don't want to hear." Actually, there was a lot I wanted to say, but it was my father's funeral. So I ignored her and let her stand in the room. They had already had breakfast. I wanted to get the preparations over with as quickly as possible. "Let me go," was all I thought. The phone at home kept ringing. My stepmother answered and whispered mysteriously in the next room. However, the time drew near, the funeral service began.

Finally Leyla came, I was relieved. Verses from the Koran were read, food was distributed and people began to disperse. My stepmother pulled me aside. She informed me that she needed an urgent operation. But there was no one she could trust with the children. Suat had to be taken to school, someone should stay with the kids. It was a problem if I stayed, but also a problem if I left. I did not know, what I should do. When I spoke to Leyla about it in a whisper, she answered me: "It is best to ask your Uncle Ferhat." So I asked Uncle Ferhat: "There is nothing you can do, they are your siblings. You'll have to watch out, who else? If you want, Leyla will come and stay with you for two days. You won't be alone here," he offered. He still didn't know about all the events that had happened. I thought he wouldn't allow it otherwise if I told him. "Help clean up, I'm outside," he said and left the house.

After I got everything squeaky clean, my stepmother said, "Well, I'm going to pack my suitcase now. I'm going to the hospital at five in the morning." It struck me as odd, why hadn't she mentioned that? This incident was also very confusing for Leyla, but we had solved the problem. That night Leyla also left me and we lay down on our floor beds to sleep. It had been a tiring day. As I was closing my eyes, the house phone rang. My stepmother answered. Who else was calling at this time? To this day, I still don't know the answer to that question. She spoke very quietly, I got up and walked closer. She covered her mouth with one hand so her voice wouldn't be heard. Since I didn't understand anything, I went back to my bedroom.

When I woke up with my stepmother in the morning and wanted to walk her to the car, she insisted, "No, stay home!" She didn't want me to go with her. A car had stopped behind the house. Since the morning was very quiet, every noise was easy to hear. My stepmother left the house with her suitcase. I wondered who picked her up and looked through her bedroom window. I didn't know this man. My stepmother got in the car and they drove away. Before she left the house, she had neither stroked nor kissed my siblings' hair. I found her leave very strange.

Both my siblings woke up. For the first time, all responsibilities belonged exclusively to me, even though we didn't know each other at all. We didn't know anything about each other. After breakfast, Suat left home to go to school. I wanted to have a good time at home with Kiraz. Kiraz was still baby, I couldn't neglect her. Even though I was at my father's house, I didn't feel at home. I was like a stranger, a guest. As my stepmother advised, I had washed Kiraz and cleaned up the house. While I was braiding Kiraz's hair, small stones were thrown at the bedroom window. I was scared, but I didn't want to show that fear.

The more I thought about this fear, the more I scared. I quietly told Kiraz to please be careful that we weren't safe here. I wanted to go out and chase them away. But I didn't know what would happen to me if I went out. I was now in charge of Kiraz. We didn't even move the curtains so they would think we weren't home. This was best for Kiraz and my safety. People were knocking on the door, they were banging on it... Suddenly I got scared, because since Kiraz was still small, she made noises every now and then that gave us away. "We know you're in there, open the door," they demanded. A rock hit the bedroom window and shattered. Frightened, I took Kiraz in my arms. I kept motioning for her to be quiet.

People went into the garden. They tried to see through the broken glass. Luckily my father had iron bars attached to the windows at the time so they couldn't climb in. But they didn't stop throwing stones. With each throw, one more piece of glass broke off. I could literally hear what they were talking about as if they were standing next to me. Kiraz was still sitting on my lap, I didn't think to take her down. On the contrary, I hugged my sister tighter. The bedroom door was open. They had already broken half the glass, one more piece, then they could even open the curtain.

The women yelled loudly from behind, "The little bitch's starting to wag her butt. The men immediately gathered around them. You were just waiting for your stepmom to leave! You turned your father's house into a brothel!" I was in great danger. Why had the villagers judged me so severely? Her words pierced my heart like a dagger, it hurt a lot. I cried again, I couldn't call anyone. "Woe! woe! Why is this happening to our village? Because of you there is no honor in our village. Let's call the police, tell them that they've turned their father's house into a brothel," her harsh words wafted in at us. My desperation grew, I sought refuge in my God. He was the only one protecting and watching me at that moment. Despicable murderous people stood outside, still trying to break the bedroom glass completely, while badly slandering me. "Open!" they roared, hungry and greedy. There were men banging on the door with all their might. God knew what I was going through in that moment and I was only fourteen years old... "Be merciful, be merciful," I begged inwardly...

Yasemin sobbed heartbreakingly during the recording and I got goosebumps listening to it. Yasemin continued her recording. She cried, shed her pain with tears, recovered and reported:

The number of people around the house increased. It was the women who made the most serious accusations. I still didn't understand it and didn't want to understand it either. I had a hard time accepting that. One person seemed to have a conscience, she said, "Shame on sinners, do you know what wrongs you are doing? Get out of here, on what days did you see something bad from Yasemin?" Those who thought so had seen what happened from afar. They didn't even say what they thought. It was tyranny. Almost an hour had passed. I was exhausted, Kiraz was shaking. She was restless. After all, our safety was at stake. A car had stopped in front of the door. I stared out in disbelief, they actually called the police saying I had turned the house into a brothel. However, it was a lie. I have been slandered. I was a child with no mother and father in my life. Many stones were thrown at me. What even my father had done after my stepmother's betrayal! So why shouldn't others do the same?

There was a knock at the door. I spoke shakily through the door: "I'm afraid I can't open the door. Can you tell the crowd to go first." "You must open, open the door, let's not say it twice." I answered quickly, "I'll open, but I'm afraid, please remove these Crowd first from my house." The crowd dispersed at that, but I could still hear their heavy insults. So I opened the door after they knocked again. "Come in, I have to close the door immediately," I begged. Apparently they didn't expect such a situation because they were surprised when they saw me. It was quickly explained why the villagers behaved like this. I said that my stepmother went to the hospital because she was going to have surgery, so I stayed at home with my siblings. I explained that my mother and father had passed away, recounted the disasters that befell me when my stepmother and Uncle Ferhat were kidnapped me. They didn't interrupt me, so I reported everything from beginning to end. While three of the police officers listened to me, the other two went through the rooms of the house one after the other. When the police saw that I was innocent, they did their best to help me. I thanked him sincerely. They even picked up Suat from school, the whole time I was afraid that something would happen to him. It wasn't until he got home that I calmed down.

Finally Uncle Ferhat came too. I opened the door, I was relieved to see him, but suddenly, in an unexpected moment, he hit me in the face with all his might. Suddenly I found myself on the floor. I covered my face with my hands and was surprised. "I didn't bring you here to lie among all the men in the village, did I? I sent you to your father's funeral. Look what you've done. You have dishonored me! I won't expect anything more from you, whatever you are from now on, you're not mine anymore," he yelled, kicking me constantly with his foot. The police intervened and they pulled him away from me by the arms. Then they took his testimony.

After a wreck, I was experiencing another one. When I experienced this fate, I had just turned 14 years old. I was crushed under the enormous weight on my tiny shoulders. This is not what my life should be like...

"Yasemin cried for almost three minutes, although the recording continued. Every time I heard her cry, I had tears in my eyes. While she was recording this for me, I was asleep in her apartment. How strange life was, how cruel life was at times. When I woke up, I didn't even realize that Yasemin was wandering these worlds, and she didn't tell me anything. This situation worried me. As Yasemin had told me, it was like reliving what she had been through. As she described it, I could picture it all clearly, as if I were witnessing it. Everything in my head was frozen, I had to process it little by little. I should take a break. Yasemin's life was very difficult and tragic at that." After recovering, I continued to listen to the recording.

"I told the police what had happened to me. Explained everything, everything I had experienced from point to point. They talked, "Are we going to take the children to the orphanage, or are we going to let them stay here?" "Call the hospital to see if their stepmother is really there?" one of the men ordered.

That question had never occurred to me. I didn't have the thought. Why would she lie? "My stepmother needed an operation, she's in the hospital," I insisted, as if protecting her. However, there was no such patient by her name in the hospital. Meanwhile, Uncle Ferhat was taken away from near the house. I didn't know where they were taking him. Everything developed way too fast. I was desperate and confused because I didn't want to be put in an orphanage with my siblings. For my siblings and my own safety, I asked the officer: "Are soldiers staying around our house to protect us?" Luckily, after long discussions, it was approved. Guards were posted around the house for two days. Inside, I still had hope that my stepmother would return home. I had to wait for them, deliver my siblings safely and go my own way. I wanted to do my duty because I knew very well what it meant to be motherless and fatherless. I had to wait so my siblings wouldn't experience that feeling. Towards evening my aunt who lives in Germany called. I told her what my stepmother had done. We chatted for about ten minutes.

She said they could bring us to Germany. I had hoped that a new door would be opened for my siblings and myself. Though I thought I was hopeless, at that moment I was happy with what she was saying.

"If your stepmother doesn't come, go to your aunt who lives in Ankara. Don't stay in this house. Call me when you get to your aunt's and we'll start the process." My other aunt also lived in Germany. She said she would speak to her too. She somehow wanted to bring us to Germany. Our phone call made me feel good. It was the first time I'd had such a hopeful conversation in months. It felt relieving. It was night. Despite the fact that we still didn't know the feeling of security, we felt safe because we were protected by the guards. What if they weren't there? Who knows what would have happened to us? God forbid! Even thinking was a nightmare because God was our only protector. We had a quiet night with a very comfortable sleep. In a way, I was also glad that I got rid of Uncle Ferhat. But I didn't know where they had taken him.

"Everyone gets punished sooner or later," I said to myself. My brother Suat left home for school early. He was very confident, but I was still concerned. My siblings and I only had to wait one more day before we would know if my stepmother was coming back. If not, we had to go our own way. When Suat was at school, I asked the soldiers, "Can we go to the hospital?

Kiraz misses her mother very much, she cries all the time."

"You can't do that without our commander's permission," I received an answer. They swore, "What the hell is this woman causing us and her birth children such troubles?" I remember asking them again. Out of pity, they then asked if it was possible to grant my wish. I don't think they would have acted the same way in any other situation. So we drove to the hospital and I personally asked the staff about my stepmother. In fact, she had never been to a hospital anywhere in the area.

I seethed with anger. She's a mother, how could she leave her children alone? It was time to turn to our own lives. When I got home I had completely different thoughts. The anger in me was even higher. I was desperate and asked my God for a better way. When I was a child, I was left alone with two children. I didn't want to believe it. The first few days were difficult, but I still had to get used to this idea. I said to myself: "You have to be patient! You will wait!" A young man brought Suat home. Thank goodness he was there, but I was very surprised. Suat cried! As soon as I opened the door, he rushed into his room. The young man asked, "Are you Yasemin?" "Yes, I'm Yasemin, who are you?" I asked.

"I'm Suat's classroom teacher," he replied. After the greeting, I let him into the apartment. But he didn't want to sit down.

He told me what happened on the way to school that they beat Suat at school and constantly hurled severe accusations and insults at him. They even inflicted injuries on him. I hurriedly told what had happened and why the gendarmerie was not protecting us. I worried that this would affect Suat's grades. "If my stepmother doesn't come home, we'll probably move out of here," I said. The class teacher was surprised and upset. "He's the top student in my class. He's very successful, smart and hardworking, it's going to hit him hard," he told me. I was upset about this situation but there was nothing I could do. Before he left he asked us to call him whenever we needed help and gave us his phone number. In addition, I was pleased to have benevolent people around us who were different from those who only helped for their own benefit.

I hoped there would always be good people around us. I kept saying to myself, "One day, you'll have to be patient until then." I had to take my siblings and go. Mainly for my own safety and for the future of my siblings. The situation called for it. Actually, I had no other option. Suat's teacher's approach gave me confidence for the moment. Suat was mad at me because of the negativity he had experienced at school. He hadn't left his room yet, he didn't want to talk to me. However, I was a victim, not a criminal, nor the perpetrator. But at that age it was not possible to understand these things.

He had heard bad words about me from his classmates and was beaten up because of it. He was angry about that and thought about me. This situation made me very sad.

"The last day in my village."

It was getting dark, evening was falling. While I was cooking, the gendarmes were still outside the door. They too were hungry and thirsty. "Come in to supper, my brothers," I begged them. However, they answered me, "We can't go in, we're not allowed." A few villagers, who saw me briefly speaking to them outside, immediately started rushing: "Look, now she's shamelessly wagging her butt in front of the soldiers." I went into the house crying, then I asked Suat to bring them food. I couldn't understand why they treated me so cruelly. To be honest, I still can't understand it today. There was no conscientious person among them to say, "This girl has not committed a sin, leave her alone." Those who thought so just watched from afar like onlookers. I think it's a sin to be silent about something like this. When there is injustice, one should not remain silent. When Suat brought out the food, they ate. That relieved me. So I sat down at the table with my siblings and then we ate too. "We'll be here until tomorrow, then we'll go," I started a conversation, because they should know what to expect.

Okay, Kiraz was still small, only three years old, she didn't know what that meant. But Suat, he was actually a healthy and intelligent child, however the repetitive negativities had also affected him psychologically. We should stand side by side, back to back, and stick together. So I talked to Suat for a long time after dinner. He was upset and crying, but in the end we hugged. After all, I was his older sister, I hadn't done anything to be ashamed of. Those who did this should be ashamed, not me. I tried to explain it to him thoroughly.

Of course he was smaller, I was a child too, but I didn't see myself as such at the time because there were too heavy loads on my shoulders to carry. I have forgotten my childhood, even as a child I was more mature than any other child. First I got Kiraz ready for bed, then Suat. He lay down on his bed but could not sleep. I looked through the curtain to the gendarmerie who were still on duty. God bless them. I wanted it to be morning as soon as possible. I cried a lot that night because I didn't know what tomorrow would bring us. We would take new steps, but I dreaded it, not knowing which ones. I prayed fervently to my God, "Lord, give us what is best for us. For my brethren and for me, lead this way, my Lord."

In the morning Suat insisted on going to school, I didn't want to stop him. I also hoped that maybe my stepmother would come back, but we had already packed everything in a suitcase to leave. The only question was, how did we get away from here? There was no car, there was no one to help us except God.

An hour later I had spoken to my maternal aunt who lived in Ankara. I wrote down their addresses and other necessary information. "Come to me, but alone," she demanded. "Don't come to my door with her children. She should be ashamed!" Somehow I didn't expect anything else from her, although the word aunt meant to me that she should take on the role of mother in an emergency. Maybe I just thought that because I lost my mother so early. I don't remember how I spent the night with excitement. The soldiers said they would stand guard outside the door until five o'clock in the evening, after which they would have to leave. But my brother Suat was in school and my stepmother still hadn't come. I was still hoping and waiting for her to step through the door at any moment.

Listen to the silent screams of a child whose life has been stolen!

Yasemin's Desperation

CHAPTER
18

The class teacher brought Suat home after school. He explained that he was very sorry because he had searched for Suat's mother in the surrounding hospitals with no result. He felt helpless. When he wanted to talk about the orphanage, I immediately cut him off and raised my voice, "I'm taking care of my brother and sister. We've already lost our parents, I don't want my siblings to suffer the same fate." Suddenly he hugged me. "Where are you going?" he asked. "My paternal aunt lives in Ankara. We'll go to them, they're waiting for us," I replied. "I'll drive you, let me take you there to make sure you arrive safely," he offered. I thanked him wholeheartedly, but declined: "Who knows what my father told my aunts. Our villagers gossip and slander me. I cannot accept your offer, sir. But I'd appreciate it if you could drive us to the bus station," I said. The teacher had told the gendarmerie that he would take us with him.

After phoning the commander, he was asked to give the gendarmerie a written and signed document confirming that he will deliver us safely. Then the gendarmerie withdrew in front of our house. The teacher suggested, "Let's meet on the main road so we don't run into the villagers. I couldn't bear it if you were called names again." I still refused his help, but he insisted, "As I said, please, I want to drive you safely to your aunt's." So he parked his car nearby of the house and we loaded the heavy suitcases.

We agreed on the time we would meet at the beginning of the main street before he drove away. Suddenly I was very excited, it felt like I was on the run. After packing our personal belongings into our backpacks, I opened the front door. My heart was beating fast with excitement. I experienced both fear and joy, two opposite feelings at the same time. I closed the door and looked back at the house one last time. It wasn't the time for emotions, I should have been strong.

Don't be afraid, woman!
No persecution goes unpunished.

CHAPTER
19

With our bags on our backs we walked along the small dirt road. Although my heart was broken, I proudly held my head up. I held Suat in my right arm and Kiraz in my left. So, step by step, we made our way into an uncertain future.

We hadn't left the village yet. It was at least thirty minutes to the main street where we would meet the teacher. But I still risked everything...

"Don't look back, keep the pace. No matter what happens, we continue on our way. We will not reply to anyone. Did you hear me?" I asked my siblings firmly. They nodded and followed my words exactly.

A villager saw how we were about to leave, he told another of our departure. What would happen now? I didn't know how many people would come. Soon everyone would know we were leaving. I stubbornly walked on, I didn't look back. "Pray, pray, our only protector is God!" I urged Kiraz and Suat, who grew frightened. "Don't be afraid, there's no reason. God is with us, he protects us. Don't let them know you're scared," I reassured her.

"The crowd behind us grew. Since I didn't look back, I didn't know how many people were behind us. From hearing, there were a lot." Keep up the pace, we show no fear, I admonished my siblings. "Pray to God, seek refuge in him, he will protect us."

They did what I said and kept going with a firm step. Your trust in me strengthened me.

Loud voices rose behind us. The children of the village ran to us. It wasn't just kids, but neighbors, ex-girlfriends and classmates were among them... I was horrified.

"Get away from here!"

"Get out!"

"You have defiled our village, get out! Get out!"

"Leave our village!"

Again, Yasemin returned to the nightmarish moments while telling the story. She kept repeating the insults and slanders that the villagers had shouted at her at the time. I listened to the recording several times in a row. I had goosebumps, it was a very scary situation that Yasemin told in tears. I couldn't understand what she had experienced, they were children, all three. We were slowly coming to the end of the recording. She had recovered from crying and continued to report:

Even if I cry, believe me, my intention is not to hurt anyone. I'm relieved, of course I feel sadness and pain, but it's good to go deep inside. You said to me, remember? "SPEAK YASEMIN, SPEAK! You will relax by speaking. YOUR SIBLINGS SHOULD NOT LIVE IN THE SAME FUTURE AS YOU HAD TO LIVE. You should yell out whatever it is that is troubling you inside. You will relax with every additional word. The cruelties will leave you, but you must not speak meaninglessly. What you say must be relevant for the future. IT HAS TO BE MEANINGFUL, VALUABLE AND IMPORTANT TO YOU. WHEN YOU REMOVE THE OBSTACLES IN FRONT OF YOU, YOU SHOULD LET YOUR INJURIES BEYOND THE SPEAKING."

"You're right, at first I felt like I'd committed a crime. Telling my story restores my confidence and it's very good for me. Also, the idea of the audio recording was great. At least the more I listen to myself, the clearer and better I recognize the injustices that have happened to me. I'm thinking about starting another audio recording after I put my siblings to bed that evening. After recording them I'll send them to you by post or maybe we'll be able to see each other again soon. I am very glad that you came to us. Please let us repeat this very often.

It was very good for all of us, I'm sorry you're going. Were you upset that I cried during the recording? Know every tear I shed brings me relief, comfort and peace. I feel like I'm tearing out this indescribable pain I've been going through. There is a lightness in me now, even if I feel a bit tired now, it was worth the effort. Thank you for everything, I'm glad you're here. "

When I heard Yasemin's last words, I took a deep breath. "Luckily you didn't leave your siblings unattended. It's good that you're there for her, Yasemin, " I said to myself. To be honest, I was a bit tired when I heard Yasemin's recording. It was also normal to be tired when hearing so many negative things. I felt sorry for Yasemin.

While Yasemin was getting ready to go to bed, she called me. "My siblings are asleep, have you arrived safely?" she asked. I said yes, then mentioned that I had listened to her recording until I met the teacher. She said, "If you have time, I'd like to tell you more on the phone. Are you okay with that? " "Of course, that would at least close a chapter," I said. "You're right, that's why I called," she replied. So she went on to say:

The villagers had literally driven us out of the village. I didn't want to believe that people could be so cruel, so cruel. It was unfair and devastating to be treated so poorly. Even the children ripped branches off the trees to chase us away.

I pulled my siblings tight to me. It was like the road would never end, it kept getting longer. We walked the path straight to the main street. We had to be patient up to this point, we had to endure the insults and curses.

Almost 26 people, young, old and also children, were waiting for us at the end of the village. We had to go through it to the main street. Apparently everyone who heard that we were leaving the village rushed over. "What have I done? What do you think about me? What have they been told? Why are they acting this way?" I cursed inwardly. Were they too blind to see that I was a victim? I was 14 years old and suffering from the mistakes of adults. They didn't leave me or my siblings alone.

About twenty meters in front of me, a 45-year-old woman raised her veil and pulled her daughter to her. She covered her eyes with her hand so she couldn't see us. Suddenly she spat at us as we passed them. After she started, the others threw twigs and small stones at us. I didn't want to have a fight with anyone in any way. We were still 150 meters from the main road. Straight on we went, under the protection of our Lord. The car wasn't in sight yet, I was alarmed. "Is he gone?" I thought. Although I wanted to leave and I was worried too.

I was afraid that they would also slander the teacher. Kiraz began to cry softly. Instead of hugging her for fear she would cry more, I encouraged her: "Wait Kiraz, wait, just a little longer and we'll be there!" When we left this road behind us, we would be begin another life. My legs were shaking badly, as were my hands and my heart... I was in very bad shape. Finally we saw my brother Suat's teacher. The car was parked at the side of the road. "Come on, run now!" I encouraged my siblings. As soon as we opened the car doors, I said emphatically to the teacher, "Come on, we have to drive fast... All the villagers are after us." Already we heard the insults and curses, people had caught up. They saw us getting in the car and started picking up rocks and throwing them at the car. Suat sat in front. When the windshield was shattered by a throw, he was injured in the forehead and was bleeding.

The crowd continued to throw rocks, ignoring that a child was injured. The main street was crowded! Thank God there was hardly any traffic on the road, so the teacher was able to drive off quickly. We were all in great shock. My legs were still shaking and I started crying. After my tears flowed, Suat and Kiraz started too. After a few kilometers the teacher stopped. "Drink some water, breathe slowly, you are in a state of great shock right now," he admonished us. But I didn't want him to stop because I was still afraid that the villagers would appear at any moment and attack us again.

However, he stopped again at the next rest stop. I remember very well how, in a loud, hectic and shy voice, I thanked him on my knees. He replied, "Shout as loud as you can in the car, you're safe here. As long as I'm with you, no one will harm you. "The last time I heard this sentence was from my mother. He was warm, reliable and sincere. My siblings and I were safe.

After I ended the phone call with Yasemin, I went to bed. This time it was me who cried. After I covered myself with the duvet, I couldn't hold back the tears. What a nightmare they had experienced on the street. Almost a week had passed. In the meantime we had made two calls. We had talked about what we had done during the day and about our working life. But I also mentioned again that she needed psychological support. "I want too, but when? I go to work and have my siblings, how is that supposed to work? If this were not the case, I would leave immediately, "she answered. If she could get a person assigned by the state to look after her siblings in her absence, she could go. But there was still the fear that the state would take away her siblings.

There were other fun conversations over the phone too, we were familiar, warm, honest and genuine with each other. After work I went home. As I opened the door, a thick envelope in my mailbox caught my eye. I was surprised, the envelope was from Yasemin, at the same time I was excited to hold another cassette in my hands. In the guest room, I sat on the couch, stretched out my feet, ready to listen to the recording. I took a deep breath, not knowing what cruelty awaited me this time.

My heart started bleeding again, after the recording with the villagers I couldn't sleep for three days. I had reopened a deep wound. I didn't have time to think about my private life while I was at work or at home taking care of the kids. However, as soon as I settled down and my siblings slept, my demons were back. But as you said, "Crying will ease the pain, the light will illuminate the darkness." On the fourth day I was upright again.

There are some wounds for which there is no ointment, it can take three days, three years or thirty years, they will never heal completely. Talking just makes it more bearable, I wasn't aware of that before. Thanks to you, I feel relieved." Anyway, let me pick up where I left off. My brother Suat's teacher was very quiet, he was excited, desperate and confused because he couldn't believe what was going on. In the restaurant he asked me to tell him everything that had happened so far. "You have to tell me everything down to the smallest detail," he demanded, it was his right! I was very hungry but we had no money. "Teacher, you brought us here, but we don't even have a lira in our pockets," I said, embarrassed. He was amazed at what I said. "That's none of your business. Let's talk more over dinner," he offered.

God bless him and those like him. Our meals were served. Even though I was hungry, I couldn't swallow a bite. Kiraz slept in my arms. Luckily Suat ate something. The teacher waited for my explanation. However, I hesitated. My throat was tight and I started to cry. The teacher was like you, he said, "Relax, cry if necessary." Just like you, he patiently waited for me to recover. Into the silence he said, "Let me tell you a little bit about myself, if you want." He didn't treat me like a child, he approached me like an adult. His sincerity inspired more confidence even though I didn't know him. I thought he was a kind-hearted person. "I like to listen," I asked him to tell.

So the teacher began to explain: "I was transferred here about ten months ago. I was born and raised in Izmir. I am 32 years old and like you I am orphaned. But my life story is different from yours because I did not know my late mother and father. I never had the chance to get to know her. I was placed in an orphanage when I was nine. My father was a manufacturer and my mother was a general secretary. I was the child of a wealthy family, but unfortunately I have no siblings. My parents' family friends have been looking for me over the years. Finally they found me. My relatives adopted me." "What do you call your adoptive parents?" I interrupted politely. "Of course they are my parents. You have many rights over me. They mean a lot to me, they made me the man I am today," he said. "Come on, please, now it's your turn, tell me what happened."

This is how I started to talk: "I was seven years old when my mother died. My father remarried two months later. As you know, I was just a kid." "You're just a kid," said Suat's teacher to me. If he knew what I went through, he wouldn't say it!

Anyway, I explained to him one by one what had happened. I told him everything. In the middle of it, Kiraz woke up, I didn't want to continue talking in front of her, so after dinner she went to the river to play with Suat, then I told him about the rape I went through, up to the unjust accusation of my father. His mouth dropped open in shock. "What power is that, what will, what determination is that that you radiate?" he kept repeating. At that moment I laughed. He was surprised that I laughed. Of course he was surprised, I didn't understand it myself. "Well, what will happen now, how will your life go on? Do you have relatives, friends far away who you know from the past? Someone who can take you in?" Taking a deep breath, I answered, "I don't know! We'll go to my paternal aunts first. What we will experience there, what we must experience, only God knows."

The teacher was very upset and deep in thought. "It's not your home. It is better for you to leave so that you can have a happy life. You must move forward, others must not pollute your life. You don't have to take on the sins of others. I will speak to my family about your situation. If anything happens, call my family immediately! Then tell them where you are. They will pick you up from there.

Now I'm taking you to your aunt. I can't drop you off at the bus station, I'll drive you to your aunt's to give me peace of mind. So I can also see how you will live. Keep me up to date," he asked me. I'm glad I opened up to him, the conversation relieved me. After my siblings came back from a walk, we drove to my aunt's. On the one hand I was getting worried because I didn't know what to expect, on the other hand I was excited.

At that time I did not think about what to do with two children of this age, how to protect them and how to raise them. Maybe I should have thought about it, but I was a kid who had had so many nightmares that I just wasn't thinking. The only thing that came to my mind along the way was that a miracle should happen. I wondered what would await us from now on, what our days should be like. Was I left to my fate again and could I fight my fate alone? I did not know it! If I had known beforehand: WOULD I EVER GO THERE? I wouldn't go absolutely.

Suat was in the front, I was in the back with Kiraz. We drove to my paternal aunt in an uncertain future...

My aunt's house was not easy to find, it was in the big city. We had driven around asking passers-by for directions. Since I went to her for the first time, I didn't know where they lived. It definitely didn't look like normal village life, I thought. We stopped in front of a slum. The teacher got out of the car and rang the doorbell. When my aunt opened the door, I immediately got out of the car. My brother-in-law also came to the door and stared at the teacher. "Sorry, I didn't introduce myself. I'm Suat's class teacher and I wanted to deliver the three of them here personally out of a sense of duty."

My aunt thanked me and we all went into the small, narrow house together. There was a living room, a bedroom, a corridor, a small kitchen and a bathroom. My aunt had no children, she was a cleaning lady and my uncle a taxi driver. Both worked in the home of a wealthy family. My aunt immediately offered the teacher, "It was a long drive. We can prepare the table, let's have dinner together." "Don't worry, I've done my duty, I'll leave immediately," he declined, asking permission. Looking at me, he added, "I'm always here for you, you can call me anytime." So we said goodbye to the teacher.

To be a woman;

it is the same in every language,

religion and every race!

CHAPTER
20

After saying goodbye to the teacher, we all went into the living room. I encountered questions that I did not expect. Her demeanor and approach were not warm. It didn't feel sincere. Their mood and gestures were more like: "Now we have to take them in too." To be honest, I was saddened by this situation. My brother-in-law said he had something to do and left the house. When he left, my aunt was warmer and approached us. Suddenly she hugs us. At that moment I realized that she was under the influence of my brother-in-law. Was she a victim herself? "Aunt, are you afraid of my brother-in-law?" I asked her. "Don't worry, niece, I respect him," she replied. She treated me like a child, I will never forget it.

"Aunt, I don't think you understand the scope of the incident. You shouldn't have called us here because you're a victim yourself. You shouldn't have put yourself and us in this difficult situation, "I said, as if holding her accountable. Yes, she shouldn't have called us. Suddenly she cried, "What if I hadn't done it? You are my brother's daughter, should I have fed you to the wolves?" Suat and Kiraz sat quietly beside me. "We have to register Suat at school. He shouldn't stay away from a school. He must not be robbed of his education. Let's go and sign him up tomorrow. I also find a job and work to contribute to the house," I said.

After that, my aunt said, "Your brother-in-law will take Suat to his place of work so that he can work too." "You can't do that! You can't do that, my brother will go to school. You won't gamble with his future," I protested. There is nothing worse than wanting to educate yourself but not being able to. They laid stones on his future. I insisted that Suat go to school. "Your brother-in-law has already decided," she replied. I was in a more complicated situation than I thought. "Now I had to face another challenge?" 'You can't do anything, you mustn't stand in front of your brother-in-law and contradict him.

You must submit to your fate. Wake up, your reputation is ruined in the village. Before it also happens here with us, you have to take your luck into your own hands and get married. This would be best for you. You are now responsible for your siblings. Regain your honor without getting into more distress in the process. Instead of being pushed around, you build your home," she said. I was amazed at this statement. I wasn't a woman, I was a child, and my situation wasn't my fault. How painful it was to hear those words. Every word she said pierced my heart like a dagger. I couldn't believe what my aunt said. "You can't do this to me. It wasn't my fault, I suffered. If these are your thoughts and plans for me, then let's go. We don't have any accommodation here either."

I said angrily. Suddenly my brother-in-law entered the house, he was carrying a bag. Because of what my aunt said about my brother-in-law, I was very afraid of him. I wish the teacher would have taken us to his family. How should I call him? They wouldn't let it. My brother-in-law was acting a bit strange, my aunt almost ran to the door and took his bag, then went into the kitchen. I thought he was shopping. But it turned out to be alcohol. I sat on the sofa, bewildered. "Your luggage is still in front of the door, get it, then go into the kitchen?" he ordered me, laughing. "No, brother-in-law, I talked to my aunt, I'll get up right away." "Women bake and clean. Go help your aunt in the kitchen!" he snapped.

He called me a woman like my aunt, I was a CHILD. I wasn't a woman, I was a child. That one word explained the way they looked at me very well. But I wasn't the person they saw. I was a victim, everything developed against my will. Why was that so difficult to understand? If they had no conscience, why were they so strict and narrow-minded.

While telling this episode, Yasemin sobbed. I felt my knees shaking as I listened to the recording over and over again. My heart was hurt, my heart ached. I continued to listen to the recording and said I hope the ending turns out well.

Desperate and sad I went to my aunt in the kitchen. "What should I do now?" As my mind wandered, my aunt insisted that I prepare sliced melon, feta cheese, spicy paste, glass, water, etc. on a tray. In the meantime she fried fish. "What do you do with jam?" she asked. I remembered it well, I replied, "I wanted to help set the table." Because I thought there was a quick breakfast for supper. "This is for your brother-in-law," she said, taking the raki out of her pocket and setting the bottle on the tray. "Come, bring it to the table, move." When I saw the bottle, I remembered the nightmarish rape incident I had witnessed. "Don't drink, please!" I begged, terrified. She got angry with me and I fled back to my master.

It was terrible for me, I didn't even want to sit in the same room with them, but the house was too small. My siblings and I didn't have the opportunity to go to another room, so we had to breathe the same air as them. They sat at the table and enjoyed themselves as if we weren't there. My aunt drank with him. My siblings were hungry and with my aunt's permission I prepared something for us.

After we satisfied our hunger, I prepared our sleeping places in the room where we were all staying. The more my aunt and brother-in-law drank, the better they felt. But I felt terrible. "Gritt your teeth, you can do it, Yasemin. You'll call the teacher's family tomorrow," I motivated myself. We couldn't stay in this house, it was a dangerous place. The TV light flickered. I was very tired, but I resisted falling asleep.

I couldn't lie down until they left the room. But they had no intention of leaving, they were in a good mood and loud, so we couldn't sleep. I sadly got up and looked in a mirror. I cried in despair, what would happen to us now, where would we go? What strokes of fate could I endure at this age? Suddenly my brother-in-law called me loudly, even though my siblings were sleeping. Why was he screaming?

After hastily washing my face, I went inside. A strange smile hit me. "Where have you been, niece? We miss you, sit down at our table, let's talk. Tell us what happened," he challenged me. "My siblings are sleeping, they might wake up! I'm exhausted too, can we talk tomorrow?" I asked. He immediately jumped up and barked at me: "Are you appealing against me?" "No, brother-in-law," I wailed. "You're making me the rules of my house, bitch!" he yelled, grabbing my hair and throwing me to the floor.

My aunt just said, "Man, why are you spoiling your mood? Enjoy yourself!" Kiraz woke up and began to cry, searching for her mother. I got up off the ground and took Kiraz in my arms. Her screams hurt me, but I couldn't do anything. My brother-in-law was still angry. "Shut her up or I'll do it," he yelled. He had awakened Kiraz after all, what an inhuman being was he? As Kiraz sat on my lap, I said softly in her ear, "Kiraz, please don't cry. Calm down my princess!

I'm with you." Fear reigned in the room, a dangerous wind was blowing. I sought refuge with my Lord. Is not our Lord, as always, our only refuge?

My brother-in-law mumbled something, he had drunk too much. I was afraid... he should go, instead he asked my aunt to pour another glass of raki.

While listening to the recording, I noticed that talking was tiring for Yasemin. Now and then she paused. It was very difficult for her to face her past.

I held Kiraz in my arms, my brother-in-law still in the room. How could I lie down tired, I leaned against the sofa, my feet drawn up. I covered us up with one hand while staring blankly at the TV. With an effort I tried to keep my eyes open because I didn't want to sleep, how could I, there were people in the room I didn't trust. I thought this night would never end. Their plates were almost empty so I hoped they would leave. Indeed, they ordered me to clear the table, then retired to their bedroom. I quickly laid Kiraz on the sofa. As they requested, I cleaned up and wiped the table. As I was washing the dishes, my brother-in-law suddenly appeared in the kitchen. I jumped back, startled, I was scared.

"Don't be afraid!" he whispered softly. He was way too close to me, he took a glass, filled it with water and tried to open my mouth with his thumb. "No, no, no, I don't want it," I whimpered. I hastily pulled my head away, but he didn't let go: "Come, drink a glass of water, your fear will go away. Why are you scared of me anyway?" He set the glass down on the counter and used his other hand to pull me towards him so I wouldn't run away. He grabbed my shoulder hard, pushed my chin up and tried to open my mouth with his thumb. No, that was out of the question. I don't know how, but somehow I managed to pull myself away from him, then ran to my siblings in the living room.

My knees were shaking, my heart was pounding like it would burst. Next to my siblings, I took a deep breath. Suat and Kiraz slept, I lay down beside them in silence. My brother-in-law turned off the kitchen light, suddenly it was dark in the house. Only his footsteps, the ticking of the wall clock and the sound of the stove filled the room. My heart was beating wildly. His footsteps seemed to be getting closer to the sofa, but I wasn't sure because I couldn't see anything.

I didn't even breathe out of fear. The bedroom door was neither opened nor closed. My brother in law was in the same room but I didn't know where. I looked around with my eyes wide open as if I could see something in the dark. I quietly pulled the covers higher and held them tight. Suddenly I felt that he was standing right next to the sofa, his hand groping for me on the covers. "Yasemin?" he whispered softly.

Although I was afraid I was brave too, because I hissed, "Take your hand away, what do you want?" I immediately jumped up and pulled the quilt towards me as if it could protect me. "Okay, don't yell, be quiet! You'll wake up your aunt and siblings," he whispered. Bad memories welled up in me, I never wanted to experience anything like that again, I waved my hands around and kicked to make him go away. "Don't worry, Yasemin, I was rude to you earlier, I just wanted to apologize. I'm going to bed now," he tried to calm me down. He searched for my body with his hands.

Suddenly Suat woke up. "Sister! Yasemin's sister!" he called to me. My brother-in-law hastily pulled his hand away, then quietly went back to his bedroom. "Yes, Suat?" I answered and added. "I'm thirsty! I was afraid to get up alone. Come with me Suat, let's go to the kitchen together." I turned my head away so he wouldn't see me crying. After I switched on the kitchen light, I made sure that my brother-in-law was really gone. Suat asked me, "Sister, how many days will we have to stay here, we won't live here, will we?" "We won't live in this house. We can't stay here. Don't tell our aunt, we have to secretly find a way to call your teacher and his family tomorrow. Don't be afraid, I'm with you!" My goal was to trust him.

In the morning my aunt woke me up by nudging me hastily.

She murmured, "Get up, get up, it's morning, you're still in bed. You can't set up a home like that. "It wasn't even six o'clock, though, and they didn't let me sleep all night. "The visit is over, get up, we have a lot of work today," she urged me on. Without protesting, I stood up in silence, only thinking about leaving and not wanting to show her what I was going to do.

There was no trace of her sour mood from last night. Before me stood a very insensitive, brutal, unscrupulous woman. 'Come on, light the fire, put the water on the fire. Take the carpets, they need a wash and the house needs a sweep," she charged. I answered her wearily: "I just got out of bed, I'll wash my face, then I'll take care of everything." "Are you going to contradict me?" she asked. She was already pulling my hair, taking off her slippers and hitting me.

My heart hurt, not from the beating, how could she be so inhuman? I went to the bathroom not wanting to cry so I gritted my teeth. I had to persevere and told myself be strong the end is near you will get out of here too. My aunt woke up Suat. In order not to show my helplessness, I pretended that nothing had happened. "Did my aunt hit you?" he asked. I hugged him quickly.

"Keep an eye on Kiraz, I'm with you. The three of us are a team from now on, you, Kiraz and I. When the three of us are one, no one can hurt us. If we don't stick together, we are vulnerable. I will find an opportunity to call your teacher today. Don't worry, we can do it too," I reassured him. It was between 8am and 8:30 am if I'm not mistaken. "I take Suat to the market, he carries the groceries for me. We will also visit a doctor to get a prescription. We'll be back afterwards. You have the household done until we come back. Brew tea and set the breakfast table!" My aunt commanded harshly. "Couldn't we come too, so we can see and get to know the area? We want to see where we're going to live," I asked. "Now isn't the time to wag your butt, you'll finish the household first," she insisted, but I didn't want to stay home alone with my brother-in-law.

He coughed and coughed, he seemed awake but still in bed. I literally begged my aunt to give us a lift so I wouldn't be left home alone with him. I hadn't even said, "Wagging your butt doesn't suit me," because the greatest danger was inside the house, in her bedroom. But how should I say that to her? She was already a person who thought negatively of me. She would slander me like everyone else did. Though I was a victim, I would be the culprit again.

My aunt and Suat left without us. I gave Kiraz milk while she drank she played clueless. My brother-in-law woke up and went to the toilet. I hastily prepared breakfast in the kitchen.

Suddenly he was standing behind me. "Good morning, Yasemin," he greeted me with half-closed eyes, then he went to the refrigerator. It looked like he still had a hangover. He took out the bottle of alcohol he bought yesterday and set it down on the counter with a bang. This noise startled me, I followed it with my eyes in a panic. He picked up a glass from the shelf and filled it almost to the brim. "Don't tell your aunt," he said, and drank the entire glass in one go, then filled his empty glass to the brim again. I was so shocked I didn't know what to do. Kiraz sat in front of the television.

The kitchen was tiny and there were iron bars in front of the windows. My brother-in-law was standing right next to the counter. I kept an eye on the door as I placed the breakfast items on the tray. The slightest movement in my direction would make me run out of the kitchen. The animal drank the entire contents of the glass in one gulp and filled it again to the brim. This time my brother-in-law was even drunker than yesterday. He just dropped the glass mug, which broke. I frantically looked for a way to escape while picking up the shards. As I squirmed around on my knees, he grabbed my arm to lift me up. "What the hell are you doing? I don't like being touched, don't touch me from now on.

Don't touch me, don't do anything I don't like!" I yelled. He quickly raised his hands and said, "Okay, okay, don't be mad at me, Yasemin, don't be mad at me." I hastily left the kitchen and ran to Kiraz. My brother-in-law just kept drinking raki without a break. My sister was still wearing her pajamas. As I was putting them on, I heard the outside door slam shut. I looked from the living room to the outside door. My brother-in-law had locked it and showed me the key. "Why did you lock the door? Open the door, open the door, open it, open the door, why did you lock it?" I yelled angrily. I repeated myself over and over in fear. Panicked, I looked at Kiraz, who knew nothing, who was still waiting for me to put her on. I was nervous, anything could happen at any moment. I cried in desperation. Suddenly I got angry with my aunt, still am. Didn't you know the partner, friend, spouse with whom you shared the same bed? How could she leave me alone with him? It wasn't even possible to climb out of the windows. Iron bars were fixed everywhere. Again I was a prisoner, a victim. My brother-in-law entered the living room drunk. Kiraz grew afraid of him. I was on alert and pretended to stare at the TV, following his every move to protect myself and Kiraz.

My aunt could come at any time. Maybe she would hit me again for not doing what she asked. But I couldn't move for fear. I prayed to God silently. "Brother-in-law, the fire is burning outside, my aunt ordered me to heat the water. If I don't heat it, she'll be mad at me," I tried to say calmly.

"What happened to your face?" he asked. "What's on my face?" I asked. "Go and look in the mirror, see for yourself," he said. When I went to the bathroom and looked at myself in the mirror, I saw a swelling on my forehead, a slightly bleeding and dried red streak was near my eyebrow and a stained spot on the upper part of my cheek. I also had bumps on my skull.

Seeing the beating marks on my face, I ran my hand over my head and felt the swelling. I was in pain but didn't think I looked that bad, I was actually still bleeding. As I looked at the tracks, I became even more determined. "We have to get out of here!" Thoughtfully I looked at the door, just as he was stepping into the bathroom. I jumped, startled. "Please open the door, uncle, open the door!" I begged him. Ignoring me, he pushed on to the sink. "I want out of here! Let me out!' I screamed. In front of me was a huge, burly man and I was a 14-year-old girl... All my attempts were in vain.

It was very small and cramped in space. He pushed me in front of the faucet and turned on the water, I resisted... "I'll wash your face, go down to the faucet!" he said. "I'll do this, please let me out of here, please!" I begged. "Why are you afraid of me? Why are you panicking so much?" he asked me.

"Let me go, make room for me, go!" I protest, pushing against him with my whole body. Of course, my strength wasn't enough, he just tilted my head towards the faucet as if his behavior was correct. I was damned. He violently washed my face with one hand three or four times in a row, then grabbed my hair and lifted my head. "Look in the mirror, Yasemin," he challenged me. I couldn't look in the mirror from crying because I didn't want to see my condition, what I was going through, in this situation.

Although he insisted and forcibly lifted my chin, I couldn't look in the mirror. Kiraz was alone next door, my aunt went to the market with Suat and left me at home with this monster. At that moment, all sorts of scenes went through my head. I fought back and still fought him. He held my hair even tighter and pulled mercilessly, his body pushing against me with all his might. No matter how hard I fought, I couldn't win. I started screaming:

"Leave it! Leave me!" but it didn't help. He held my hands tightly behind my back. "Let me go, brother-in-law, please let me go!" I cried through tears. He covered my mouth with one hand while continuing to push with his body. I could feel his skin and his foul breath. I was in the same situation again, I was the victim again, I was raped again. Even though he kept my mouth shut so my voice wouldn't be heard, I didn't give up the resistance. But what's the use, I was raped. My brother-in-law raped me...

Kiraz's crying sounds reached us from outside. My unheard screams were stifled by my brother-in-law's hands during the rape. The door of the house was also locked, then my crying stopped, I was frozen... I felt neither pain nor heartbreak, my God. I died that day! My death was that day. My brother-in-law pulled up his pajamas after he was done and left the bathroom. I dropped where I was exhausted, I collapsed. I was devastated and could not get up even when the outer door was opened, I could not move. Kiraz kept crying, she couldn't come to me, nor could I reach Kiraz... I don't know how to describe this fall I experienced. Today I can say it was a shock, a total breakdown. My feelings are gone, my feelings are dead, how was a living dead.

How can this situation be explained? The ability to cry, to scream, to be in pain... I felt like I had lost all my feelings. I had even lost the strength to resist him afterwards. May God not let me experience those days again. If that were the case today, I would hurt him and leave the house. Or would have rushed to the neighbors, I would scream. I will never forget that I was frozen, I just sat still on the floor for about half an hour, focused on a single point.

How could I forget this scene, eh? My aunt would be here any minute, I should have got up, taken a deep breath and told her everything. I looked in the mirror and wanted to smash it in anger. I hated that person in the mirror, I hated being a victim. I faced my destiny over and over again. "Why, why, why?" I yelled in vain. Everything was empty... I made Kiraz cry with my screams. "I should have controlled myself!" I had to pull myself together to keep from falling apart. My siblings were younger than me. If I didn't intervene now, what would happen, what other catastrophes would we face? When I looked in the mirror this time, I stopped crying. Full of ambition and a lot of strength, I stepped out of the bathroom. My anger knew no bounds, I will fight. Kiraz immediately rushed to me when she saw me. I had a brother and a sister who needed me, I couldn't be weak. So I finished Kiraz, although I was in shock, I took out the suitcases and packed. I wanted to be done by the time my aunt and Suat returned.

That villain, that beast, hadn't left the bedroom after he raped me. I didn't care either, I risked everything, everything. Really everything... When Suat and my aunt came, our suitcases were outside the front door and I was waiting for them. Suat had too much weight in his hands, he could hardly walk. I quickly ran to him to relieve him of the heavy burden. When our eyes met, I was eye to eye with my aunt. "Are you really my real aunt?" I asked. "Of course, what does that mean? I am your biological aunt! Look at your face Come in, you want to embarrass me in front of the neighbors?" she asked. "We're not going in, we're going," I answered firmly, with determination. I was in a miserable state. I was able to do anything. All! My aunt didn't even come to us when my mother was alive. I asked my father before he married my stepmother, "Why don't my aunts come to us?"

"They don't understand each other. Your mother was kind, she suffered a lot from your aunt. One day I said enough was enough. You mustn't come any more," my late father replied at the time. He who has fallen into the sea embraces a snake to survive! This saying was really true when we went to my aunt's. A beautiful and appropriate saying. When I told her that, she angrily threw us out of the house.

Silence; quiet is acceptance.
Reticence!

Yasemin's Desperation

CHAPTER
21

I hadn't even thought about where we were going, what we should do now. We were just relieved. We had to take shelter with those heavy suitcases and find a phone as soon as possible, but where? "You come to the market from here, sister," said Suat, who had a good memory.

There were about 20 lira in my pocket, we had to make a phone call and also eat something. So we entered a small restaurant. Our condition was very noticeable, there were wounds all over my face, I was holding our suitcases and two small children by my hand. While we were drinking our soup, an old man came to our table. "Children, is there a problem? How do you look? You're not from here, have you just arrived?" he asked us. Suat asked me: "Tell him sister!"

"Uncle, can I use your phone?" I asked him. "Of course my child," he replied. "Look my children, you are in trouble, obviously you have a problem, I could be your grandfather, do not hesitate. I have returned permanently from abroad. I am retired and staying at my grandson's restaurant. My wife died, I have good days and bad days with my grandchildren. Come on, don't hesitate, tell me your problem. But if you want, call first."

"While the elderly gentleman brought the phone, we talked about how he was a good person. How do we thank our Lord?

The old uncle didn't leave us alone, either, when I called the teacher's number and spoke to him. I told him everything but not about the rape, I couldn't. When I gave him the address of the restaurant, he warned us not to leave until his family came.

As soon as I hung up, the older gentleman called out: "Set the table well for the children." Even after I protested that we couldn't ask for that, he didn't give up: "Eat, my children, don't hesitate." It was very embarrassed but we were hungry to be honest. It was noon and we had last had dinner the day before.

After about 20 minutes, the teacher called the restaurant. They brought me the phone. "Yasemin, keep an eye on your siblings, but get away from them a little now," he asked me. So I did what he said. After a few questions he asked, I started crying. His questions were endless and I didn't wait for him to finish and say it out loud: "My brother-in-law raped me!" There was silence. While I thought no one but Suat's teacher could hear me, the old gentleman heard me. I started crying, my knees were shaking, they just wouldn't stop.

I pretended to be strong in front of my siblings, but I was exhausted. "Yasemin, I'm coming, don't worry, you're not alone. We will file a criminal complaint. There is the law, there is the law, trust the law! No one can have someone by force. You're not alone. My family will be with you soon," he promised. "Don't go away, eat your food." After I hung up, the elderly gentleman said to me, "I had a feeling something was wrong, my child." My head was on the table, unable to answer, and I waited on the teacher's family."

Just as I thought we were saved, I started crying at the table. I shed many tears in silence so that others would not notice my silent screams. But I was tired of crying, just what else could I have done.

"From now on I'm your grandfather! Come whenever you want, it's yours now," said the old gentleman sadly. A couple walked in and looked around. I wondered if it was them. The couple came to our table with three children. We got up immediately.

With a smile on her face, she asked in her warm voice, "Yasemin?" I answered shakily, "Yes, I'm Yasemin."

"Suat, hello my child, how are you?" she asked Suat. "I'm fine, thanks," he said, confused. The gentleman in the suit is very polite and gentle. 'Please sit down, go on eating. Don't disturb your comfort. Have a sit my love. I'll ask the driver to get the secured child seat out of the trunk for our little sugar girl,' he explained.

Her reliable, calm, warm and sincere manner relieved me. The beauty of their hearts was reflected in their faces, and they were very well groomed and distinguished. At that moment, I felt a little ashamed of my outfit.

"If you stop eating, I'll have them clear the table. Good times await," he said. I didn't even know their names and I didn't know what to call them. I was embarrassed and hesitated. If we had met under different circumstances, I could have approached them with the warmth and sincerity they deserved. But the situation was different. Too much had happened.

The elderly gentleman was very happy for us. As we parted, he said heartily: "May my grandchildren be well. Come back, don't forget what your grandfather said," he said and said goodbye. In the meantime, our suitcases were put into a car. Kiraz received a special child seat. Before we even got in the car it was clear how thoughtful, sensitive and caring our safety was. So I and my siblings finally felt safe.

"You will be fine. Your rooms are now being prepared. When we get home it will be ready by then. First we visit the house. You'll see what's where. Look kids, you got through bad days. We must work together as a team and care for your health, happiness and peace.

We will be a team. Only then can we walk hand in hand towards peace. For your information, our family friends will be with us in the evening due to the negative experiences you have had. Suat my child, you know your teacher is my son, right?" she asked.

"Yes," he replied. "He's on his way home now, pray he gets there safely. Our family friends will be with us tonight. professor Dr. Nizamettin Koç and psychiatrist Ms. Nalân. You may find it difficult to speak at first, perhaps you do not want to speak. But so that we can move forward, we take our first steps professionally."

Mrs. Filiz wanted our well-being, she was multicultural and her heart was full of love. She wanted the best of everything for all of us. In addition, she was very well-groomed and beautiful. She is still before my eyes. She was a wonderful woman in every way, perfect in heart, face, humanity and character.

"We're getting closer to our house," she said with a smiling face and loving eyes. It was a beautiful place. I looked out the window with admiration. I was fascinated ...

Was paradise such a place? Had God sent these two angels to us and opened the gates of paradise to us? Or was it a dream I had during my long sleep that took my consciousness after the severe beatings I received?

Where was I?

Was it real or a dream? I was lost!

The End

While life sometimes offers drop by drop of happiness,
sadness rains down on us like a waterfall.
Sometimes happiness hides in sadness.
It's about seeing the miracle in the darkness
and learning with it...

Nurgül Sönmez

READER COMMENTS

Hello Mrs. Nurgül. I am writing this message to thank you. Thank you for your courage to write about today›s topics. Don›t deviate from the way you do it. We love you.

Hatice ÖZDEMİR

Hello dear author. I am writing you this heartfelt message. I have just finished your book. It took me some time to come to my senses, but in the end I wanted to write to you. You covered such a topic! It is not easy to write about these subjects. I congratulate you on your courage, I congratulate you. I hope you never stop writing. Thank you.

ANONYM

First, I really want to thank you. You raised such a beautiful topic! These are the wounds that still bleed today. I am very sorry for what Yasemin went through, I was very touched. It doesn›t fit into words, only those who read will understand me. Kudos to your work. I wish you continued success and will see you again in many more of your books. With love."

Gaye HANIM

Oh Nurgül, I can›t believe you. You wrote a really great book. I couldn›t put it down. I don›t know how the hours have passed. Health for your heart, for your pen. I look forward to your new books. Kind regards.

Saime ÖZAK

Ms. Nurgül, you are simply wonderful. I want to give you a special congratulations on bringing such a useful book to society. I hope the beauties you made will come back to you more than once. Respect.

ANONYM

Dear Hello, Ms. Nurgül. I am writing from Kocaeli. I wasn›t a book reader. I bought your book for no reason at the fair I attended with my friends. Glad I bought it. I think it›s one of those books that you absolutely have to read before you close your eyes forever. I hope we have the opportunity to meet face to face one day. May your pen be permanent.

Asım BEKGÖZ

Writing isn>t for everyone. In particular, writing important to-pics requires great courage. I congratulate you very much, you are doing a great job for society. With my endless thanks.

İlhan KONUR

Dear Author. I bought your book from the fair. I have read a lot of your books on the internet. As soon as I got home I opened it and started reading. What you wrote about a suffering girl is also a true story that touches me deeply. Your book tells so many facts... I was very sad while reading it. I wish you continued success.

Saide BAKIR

Hello Ms. Nurgül. An award-winning book. OSCAR ripe! You stuck your head in a problem that affects the world, not the cultural one but a worldwide problem. Child labor, child bride, abuse, violence… Whatever you are looking for. You have touched the bleeding wound of the world. I wish that it will be translated into every language. You have such a beautiful narration that reading it made me feel like I was wat-ching a movie. I like her style very much. Both the series and the movie could be made for your book. I congratulate you. I hope it gets into the hands of the right person and that we will see your book at the highest level. I wish you success. Kind regards.

Levent GÜMÜŞ

You are the most beautiful person I have ever known. It is the most touching book I have read in my life and will never be forgotten. I wish you continued success. I cried so much while reading the book, I was so touched. I can recommend it to everyone. No Yasemin should have to suffer anymore in the future. You are also a great writer. May God always open the way for you. Let›s no longer be silent for all the Yasemins in the world.

Gülizar KÜÇÜK

I›ve been looking for you a lot on social media. It›s been two weeks since I read your book. I›m still under the influence and when asked, I›ll say, «You guys feel the emotions that an amazing book gave me». I recommend your work, which I find successful. Health for your hand, for your heart, dear author. Respectfully."

Tamer ÇETİN

Hello Mrs Nurgül. After I started reading your book, I finished it in three days. It›s very haunting. I also liked that you give a cut of the book›s income to the needy orphans. There are thousands of Yasemins around the world who have been subjected to this abuse and left as victims. God help you. I wish you continued success."

ANONYM

Hello, Ms. Nurgül. I got to know and read your book through my daughter. It is commendable that you present your readers with a carefully studied work. I congratulate you from the bottom of my heart. The voice of one Yasemin out of thousands of Yasemins reached your readers. God bless your heart and pen that let us hear that unheard voice. May your success be forever.

ANONYM

Really, I›m someone who hates reading books and I›m ashamed of it. However, your book is so lifelike that I couldn›t put it down while reading it. It was a life that had already been experienced, a suffering life. Not from a normal life, it was a painful life. Thank you for presenting such work. "

ANONYM

I finished the book in two days. Now it›s time for the second book. I›m glad I met you at the fair in Ankara. I read a very good book.

ANONYM

Hello Ms. Nurgül. It was the most meaningful and touching book I have ever read. I promise it won›t get lost among my other books. The place will always be special to me. I wish you continued success in your writing life. Goodbye. "

ANONYM

Matilda Türkçe

Savaşın İçinden Bir Kelebek

Sert Kapak - İnce Kapak - e-kitap

Matilda Deutsch

Ein Schmetterling inmitten des Krieges

Paperback - Hardcover - e-book

Matilda English

A butterfly through the war

Paperback - Hardcover - e-book

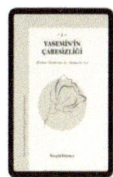

Yasemin'in Çaresizliği - 1 Türkçe

Binlerce Yasemin'den Bir Yasemin'in Sesi

Sert Kapak - İnce Kapak - e-kitap

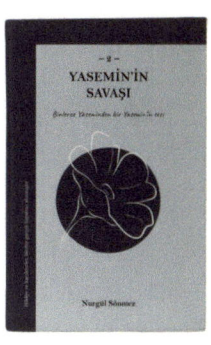

Yasemin'in Savaşı - 2 Türkçe

Binlerce Yasemin'den Bir Yasemin'in Sesi

Sert Kapak - İnce Kapak - e-kitap

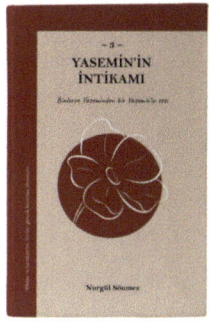

Yasemin'in İntikamı - 3 Türkçe

Binlerce Yasemin'den Bir Yasemin'in Sesi

Sert Kapak - İnce Kapak - e-kitap

Yasemins Verzweiflung - 1 Deutsch

Eine Stimme unter Tausenden

Paperback - Hardcover - e-book

Yasemins Kampf - 2 Deutsch

Eine Stimme unter Tausenden

Paperback - Hardcover - e-book

Yasemins Rache - 3 Deutsch

Eine Stimme unter Tausenden

Paperback - Hardcover - e-book

 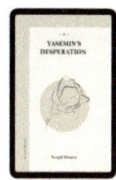

Yasemins Desperation - 1 English

One voice among thousands

Paperback - Hardcover - e-book

 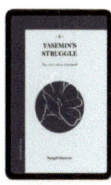

Yasemins Struggle - 2 English

One voice among thousands

Paperback - Hardcover - e-book

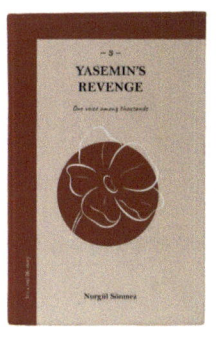 

Yasemins Revenge - 3 English

One voice among thousands

Paperback - Hardcover - e-book

1001 Gece Yerine Bin Bir Gün Türkçe

"Özgürlüğe süzülen bir mülteci"

Sert Kapak - İnce Kapak - e-kitap

Statt 1001 Nacht - Tausendundein Tag Deutsch

"Weg in die Freiheit"

Paperback - Hardcover - e-book

Instead Of 1001 Night – One Thousand and One Day English

"A refugee soaring to freedom"

Paperback - Hardcover - e-book

Maarouf Türkçe

"Vatanı tarafından terk edilmiş bir adamın, inanılmaz öyküsü"

Sert Kapak - İnce Kapak - e-kitap

Maarouf Deutsch

"Ein Mann, der von seiner Heimat verlassen wurde"

Paperback - Hardcover - e-book

Maarouf English

"The incredible story of a man abandoned his homeland by force"

Paperback - Hardcover - e-book

Teklif ediyoruz:

Almanca, İngilizce, Fransızca ve Türkçe dillerinde
uzman edebi kitap çevirileri.

. Editörlük
- Almanca, İngilizce, Fransızca, Türkçe

. Düzeltme
- Almanca, İngilizce, Fransızca, Türkçe

Nous offrons :

Des traductions littéraires professionnelles
de livres en allemand, anglais, français et turc.

. Lectorat
- Allemand, Anglais, Français, Turc

. Lecture de correction
- Allemand, Anglais, Français, Turc

Eserlerinizden çevirmekle
ilgileniyor musunuz?
O zaman lütfen bize bir
e-posta gönderin.

MERHABA — HALLO

HELLO

nurgulsonmez
ns.nurgulsonmez@gmail.com
nurgulsonmezofficial

- **Sunduğumuz hizmetler:**

Almanca, İngilizce, Fransızca ve Türkçe dillerinde uzman edebi kitap çevirileri.

- Editörlük - Almanca, İngilizce, Fransızca, Türkçe
- Düzeltme - Almanca, İngilizce, Fransızca, Türkçe

Siz de eser(ler)inizin çevirisini yapmak ve ek hizmetlerimizden (redaksiyon, düzenleme, kitap kapağı tasarımı, illüstrasyon & kitap dizgisi) yararlanmak istiyorsanız bize ulaşın.

➢ Talebinizi bize e-posta ile gönderebilirsiniz.

- **Nous offrons:**

Des traductions littéraires professionnelle des livre en allemand, anglais, française et turc.

- Lectorat - Allemand, Anglais, Français, Turc
- Lecture de correction - Allemand, Anglais, Français, Turc

Vous êtes également intéressé par la traduction littéraire de votre ou vos œuvres et par le bénéfice de nos services complémentaires (relecture, correction, conception de couvertures de livres, illustration et composition de livres).

➢ Alors envoyez-nous votre demande par e-mail.

■ Wir bieten:

In den Sprachen Deutsch, Englisch, Türkisch und Französisch fachgerechte literarische Buchübersetzung an. Zusätzlich;

- Lektorat - Deutsch, Englisch, Türkisch, Französisch
- Korrekturlesen - Deutsch, Englisch, Türkisch, Französisch

Sie haben auch Interesse Ihr Werk oder Ihre Werke literarisch zu Übersetzen und von unseren zusätzlichen Dienstleistungen zu profitieren (Lektorat, Korrekturlesen, Buchcover Design, Illustration & Buchsatz).

  Dann schicken Sie uns Ihre Anfrage per Email.

■ We offer:

Professional literary book translation in German, English, Turkish and French.

- Editing - German, English, Turkish, French
- Droofreading - German, English, Turkish, French

You are also interested in literary translation of your work(s) and benefit from our additional services (Editing, droofreading, book cover design, illustration & book typesetting).

  Then send us your request by email.